TJ *and the*
MAGIC
PENCILS

H. BARRY KAHL

First Edition, June 2018
ISBN – 13: 978-0692130551
ISBN – 10: 0692130551

This book is a work of fiction. Characters, incidents, or places are either the product of the author's imagination or used fictitiously, and any resemblance to actual persons, living or dead, events, or places is entirely coincidental.

Book Cover Design by Extended Imagery

DEDICATION

For Thomas Joseph (TJ) Barbieri

Forever you will be remembered

CONTENTS

Chapter 1
Prank

The prank seemed like a good idea at the time.

TJ and his brothers and sister were at their favorite play area, an abandoned field just past the McAllister's farm. David, his older brother, was working on the skateboard ramp that they had been building for the past two weeks. As the artist in the group, TJ was going to paint designs on the ramp as soon as David finished securing the wooden board to the metal support system. TJ had his paint and brushes and wanted to start, but David was taking his time to be sure the ramp was safe. TJ grew impatient.

"Is the ramp ready? Is the ramp ready?" he asked repeatedly.

"No! Quit asking, it's like you have ants in your pants," replied David.

TJ decided to teach David a lesson. While David was bent over, TJ dropped sand in the back of his pants. "Oh yeah, who has ants in their pants now?"

It was those words that started the fight.

"I'm gonna get you, TJ!" twelve-year-old David hollered. Stephen and Matthew, his twin brothers who were nine, joined the chase. All three were bigger than TJ. Eleven-year-old TJ had red hair, brown eyes, and a slight build, like his mother and sister. His brothers all had dark brown hair and olive skin, and were built taller and broader, like their father. With all three brothers coming after him, TJ had only one option: to run for his life.

TJ raced all the way home, went straight to the kitchen, and hid in the pantry. He found and ate most of the chocolate chip cookies his mom had made for dessert that night.

Mom opened the pantry door to grab some noodles. Her eyes widened at the sight of her son. "TJ, why do you have crumbs and chocolate all around your mouth?"

TJ figured silence was his best response.

"TJ, if you just ate all the cookies I baked today, I am going to turn into the crazy lady!" Mom said.

TJ and his siblings knew to get to their rooms before Mom turned into the crazy lady and started swinging the spatula around the kitchen. TJ scrambled from the corner of the pantry and ran upstairs. The other Binder children, who had just gotten home, thundered behind him and scattered to their own rooms, slamming their doors. Claudia, his sister and the baby of the family, was the only one talking to him at dinner time. TJ figured that the others were still furious, not just about getting them in trouble, but risking the fact that they could be punished over the next few days and would not get to keep working on the skateboard ramp and skateboards. They had labored so hard to make them from leftover and recycled items.

After everyone was finished dinner, TJ's parents assigned chores. Claudia, Stephen, and Matthew, had to clear dishes. David and TJ had to wipe the table and chairs.

"Kids, it is your job to get along and not fight with one another," Dad said. If you have a disagreement, figure it out, or tell an adult before it turns into a battle."

Mom said, "TJ, since you started the fight, and since you ate my cookies, you can go around and collect the trash from the bedrooms, bathrooms, and kitchen, and take it outside to the curb. In addition, you will not get dessert tonight. Everyone else can have ice cream sandwiches."

TJ finished wiping the table and chairs with David. By the time they were done, TJ knew he had about an hour before sunset. If he could get outside before dark, he could scrounge around for other people's recyclables. He never knew what he might find; people discarded very cool stuff!

Chapter 2
Trash

It was mind-boggling how much trash a family of seven could generate in the course of a week. Every time TJ had trash duty, he noticed Claudia's can was filled with the most garbage. What do girls do that makes so much trash? he wondered, as he emptied the container in her room. He glanced in and saw gobs of tissues, cotton swabs, an empty lip gloss tube, tea bags, dental floss, cotton balls with fingernail polish all over them, and a slew of Band-Aid wrappers. "Geez, how does she even know how to use all this stuff when she's only seven?" he mumbled. "And what is with the Band-Aids? I don't remember her getting any cuts."

When he looked across the room he saw her two favorite stuffed animals—Cuddles the bear and Queen Betty, a stuffed tiger—seated on chairs around a table set for tea. Cuddles was covered in Band-Aids.

Then TJ remembered that Matthew had used Cuddles as a defensive shield when he was kickboxing with David a few days ago. Poor Claudia, she is either going to grow up to love us or hate us, he thought, shaking his head.

TJ finished collecting the trash around the house, tying off two large white plastic bags. He dragged them from the kitchen out through the garage door. As he continued down the long driveway, he quickly scanned the other houses on the street for any obvious discarded items that might be useful. Not seeing anything, he realized he would have to walk from house to house to get a closer look.

Looking through other people's trash was a common pastime for the Binder children. This habit was not because they were poor or did not have a lot of toys. In fact, most people would probably think they were pretty lucky. They lived in a nice two story home. They had two parents who, even though they got frustrated sometimes, truly loved their children and would do anything for them. They generally got most things they requested, although they typically had to wait for a special occasion, such as a birthday or Christmas, for a bigger gift or toy.

However, every once in a while, when the kids would request a certain item, they would be told no, not even for Christmas or their birthday. Some of the items permanently banned from the Binder household were b. b. guns, nunchucks, Chinese fighting stars and, most recently, skateboards. After eight trips to the emergency room in the past year alone, TJ and his siblings had been told certain items were not worth the trouble.

It was the ban on these toys that had prompted the children to start looking through trash. Not willing to take "no" for an answer, they became resourceful and decided to create and make those items that had been forbidden. Unfortunately for Mom and Dad, the children, David in particular, were creative and talented enough to figure out how to build or make almost anything.

The b. b. gun craving had been satisfied by a slingshot David made from a tree branch and an unusually large rubber band one of the boys found in a wastebasket at school. The nunchucks were built out of a pair of discarded drumsticks from the trashcan of the older boy who lived down the street, and part of a dog leash they found in the trash at a house around the corner. Although they tried, they never found a way to make a Chinese fighting star out of anything but paper, but that was probably a good thing.

The most recent refusal of their parents to allow them to have skateboards had been dealt with by everyone pitching in. The skateboard bases were built with wooden planks the twins had found by the creek. The wheels for the skateboards had come off of some old roller skates TJ and Claudia found in a neighbor's trash. David showed his siblings how to sand down the top and sides of the wooden planks to make the board. While the others worked on smoothing the skateboard bases, David figured out how to attach the wheels.

To give David some ideas for how they could make a skateboard ramp, TJ started drawing designs based on additional scraps they had found. The smooth side of the ramp was an old billboard sign that someone had dumped in the creek along with the wooden planks. The support for the ramp came from a metal bookshelf that David found in a trash pile in front of a house someone had vacated.

Together David and TJ took worked to build the image TJ created. They took apart the bookshelf and used the parts to prop up the ramp, and reinforce and brace the back. They positioned the billboard sign on the metal pieces. Then, they secured everything with nails and screws David found in his father's tool box and around the garage.

This evening, TJ was not looking for anything specific in the trash, but thought it would be a good idea to check anyway. It was like a treasure hunt! TJ swaggered a little, like a pirate, as he headed to Ms. Watkins' house.

Mrs. Watkins was an older woman who was always making arts and crafts. Twice a year she would load up her car with the flower arrangements, baskets, hanging decorations and other knick-knacks she'd made, and head off to the state craft fair. She would always call Mom in advance and reserve the two older boys to help her load everything into the back of her car. It was a tedious process for the boys with Ms. Watkins constantly reminding them, "Be careful with that, it's *very* fragile." TJ and David tolerated the hour of aggravation because, when they were done, she would let them select a soda of their choice from the refrigerator in her garage, and hand them a delicious chocolate cake to take home for dessert. Ms. Watkins was a fantastic baker and her chocolate cake was famous at the Binder house.

Looking over her trash pile this evening, TJ only saw a few disappointing fake flowers and some picture hanging wire. He picked it up for David, but left the flowers behind. Mother's Day had passed and his mother's birthday was not until December. He did not feel like looking at pink fabric roses for the next six months.

It was a disappointing start, but TJ was in no hurry to go back home where he would be stuck inside. Deciding to venture a little further, he stuffed the wire in his pocket and continued on his way. He cut over one street, jumping the fence between the Peterson's backyard and the Borra's backyard. The Borra's house faced Colesville Street where he could usually find some hidden treasures.

About three houses down on the right he saw a huge trash pile that looked like someone was either moving or had just cleaned out their garage. He casually walked over to get a closer look.

At the bottom of the pile were a dusty old dresser, a wobbly table, and a worn sofa. Man, if we had a clubhouse this sofa would be perfect, TJ thought. Knowing a clubhouse was not something that was likely to happen for a while, he focused his search on smaller items. He began looking through one box labeled *Uncle Harry*. TJ had no idea who Uncle Harry was, but he hoped he had some good loot. The inside of the box contained a disappointing variety of books, a measuring tape, a container of old buttons, and a rusty typewriter. TJ grabbed the measuring tape, putting it in his other pocket, and took out the container of buttons, placing them on the ground. He thought the buttons would be great ammunition for the slingshot. Leaving the books and the typewriter, he placed the box on top of the wobbly table and looked through the box beneath it labeled *Aunt Margaret*.

Aunt Margaret must have loved the beach because inside the box were dozens of seashells. Most were broken or cracked. There were also a few girlie items like a brush and comb, and some make-up. He thought about Claudia for a minute, but the items were so dusty and dirty he could not imagine Claudia wanting anything to do with them. He put the Aunt Margaret box on the wobbly table next to the Uncle Harry box. Quickly, he went through the drawers of the dresser, finding an old toy army tank and helicopter. He did not feel like carrying them home, but knew that Stephen and Matthew would love them. He pulled them out of the drawer, placing them on the ground next to the button container. Realizing he better get home, he decided to put the boxes back where he found them and get moving.

As he turned to lift the Aunt Margaret box, he accidently knocked the Uncle Harry box over, causing its contents to spill on the ground. Oh man, he thought. With a sigh, he reached down to pick up the books and typewriter, and noticed a rectangular black box, still closed and lying on the curb. How did I miss this? he wondered.

He picked up the hard plastic box, marveling that it hadn't opened during the fall.

A message was etched into the top which read, *Warning: For Real Artists Only*. Real artist, he thought. Well, that definitely describes me. He easily removed the top and opened the box, revealing a collection of pencils. At first glance, they looked like ordinary black pencils with regular lead in the tip. TJ picked one out to examine it more carefully. As he touched it, his fingers tingled and he suddenly felt the urge to put everything down and draw. He brought the pencil up closer to his eyes and noticed that the tip was not the same color as that of a regular pencil. The tip looked as though it had many shades of blue all swirled together. Cool, thought TJ. When he turned it, he saw that a word was printed on the side: *Water*. Intrigued, he wanted to turn each pencil over and see exactly what was written on each, but it was starting to get dark and the last thing he wanted was to get into more trouble. Quickly, he placed the pencil back in the box and replaced the lid, making a mental note to look at the pencils more carefully later. Right now he had to focus on getting home.

Jumping the fence was not an option with all the goods he was carrying. Instead, he walked up Colesville Street, turning right onto

Maple Road. After about three houses, he turned right again, coming back down his street, Melody Lane. He was moving along, his arms laden with his container of buttons, the miniature army tank and helicopter for Matthew and Stephen, the box of pencils, as well as the metal wire and measuring tape in his pockets for David. He felt proud of his collection of items. Trying not to spill or drop anything, TJ paused in front of Ms. Watkins' driveway to readjust everything in his arms and grab a fabric rose for Claudia He now had a little something for everyone.

The sky was dark when TJ stood back up and looked down the street. In the street lights, he saw his father's truck pulling out of the driveway. Oh man, he's coming to look for me. TJ's heart skipped a beat in panic. Please don't let him see me, he thought, realizing he had taken too long outside. Much to his relief, his father headed off in the opposite direction. Deviously, he thought, Well that gives me time to sneak into the house and get this stuff upstairs before he finds me. And he quickly hurried home before his father's car had a chance to turn around.

Once he got inside he went straight upstairs, carefully balancing his loot so he did not drop anything. All the bedroom doors were closed, which indicated that his siblings were in their beds for the night. As he opened his own door, the only light came from the lamp on his desk. David was already in his bed, but not fully asleep.

"Did you find anything good out there? You were gone forever," David said as TJ opened their closet to unload his findings.

"I found a few things. I can show you tomorrow," TJ said, suddenly feeling tired.

"Sounds good," David mumbled as he turned to face the wall and drift off to sleep.

TJ changed into his pajamas, turned off the lamp on his desk, and climbed in his own bed. The pencils would have to wait until the morning.

Chapter 3
Rain

When TJ woke up that morning and looked outside, he saw nothing but pouring rain. He knew there was no way they were going to work on the ramp. He thought about going back to sleep, but noticed David was already out of bed. He figured he should probably head downstairs and see what the other kids were up to. This was the first rainy day of the summer and he predicted Matthew would try to convince everyone to play *Monopoly.* Although he liked it, *Monopoly* could last forever and the last thing TJ wanted was to be stuck at the kitchen table all day, or not have anyone to play with because everyone else was stuck at the kitchen table.

Downstairs, his siblings were awake and eating cereal. They did not notice him as he walked into the kitchen, overhearing their conversation. It did not take him long to figure out what was going on. As he'd guessed, Matthew was pushing for a game of *Monopoly*, but he seemed to be having trouble getting the others to go agree.

"I'll play *Monopoly* if you'll play tea party first," Claudia offered.

Matthew completely ignored his sister's suggestion, and turned instead to David saying, "Come on, you can be the wheelbarrow and I'll let you go first."

"That game lasts forever. I don't want to be stuck at the kitchen table all day," David said, eating his cereal. He did not look up, but kept his eyes focused on the pull-out flyer for the hardware store that was in front of him.

"Yeah, and if he gets the wheelbarrow and first roll, then what's in it for the rest of us?" TJ asked, startling everyone.

Matthew turned around to see TJ. "You don't even like the wheelbarrow, you always pick the dog. Besides, I thought you were sleeping until noon; the game would be over by then."

"I want the wheelbarrow just so David can't have it," TJ said, smiling at David. David made no reply except to roll his eyes and keep on reading. "And if you are promising the game will end at noon, you must mean noon tomorrow. David's right, that game takes forever."

"Good morning Thomas Joseph!" Claudia gushed. "I'm glad you're awake. Do you want to come to my tea party?"

TJ walked past his sister, rumpling her hair, "Maybe later, it's a little early in the morning for a party."

Stephen finally took a breath after gobbling down three bowls of cereal so fast it looked like he was in a contest with someone, and said, "Let's play Bank."

"Hooray! I love Bank! I'm buying the sofa cushions," Claudia said.

The game Bank was a Binder family original. Most of the credit went to Stephen who contrived it as a way to justify getting his hands on all the money from the board games in the house. Stephen loved money. He had saved every penny he had ever earned or gotten. He was always worried that someone might take his real money. So with Mom's help, he kept it hidden in an old hair color box that was lined with cotton balls and placed on the top shelf of his parent's linen closet in their bathroom. None of the boys would ever think to look through their mother's personal items in the bathroom, and Claudia, who might be inclined to snoop, could not reach the top shelf even with the step stool.

With his own money hidden away, playing Bank provided Stephen with an opportunity to manage and do transactions with all the fake money in the house, as though it were real. Originally, the goal of Bank was to get the most money and/or "buy" the most furniture in the house. Stephen served as the banker and would give each child a starting fund. Then they would go around and ask how much certain items cost. Stephen would give them a price and they could buy it from the Bank. Each child could pretend to have temporary ownership of the items they bought for the rest of that day. The other kids did not care about the financial aspect of the game, but played because they liked the idea of owning stuff in the house.

There were a couple of problems with the original game. The first was that as the banker, Stephen had the most money at the end of every game and always declared himself the winner. This did not sit well with the other kids who disliked losing every time the game was played. The second problem was that fights broke out because someone "owned" something that someone else needed or wanted. The game was revised and the new objective was to build the best fort using only the furniture and other materials that you bought with your money. Stephen was okay with this because he still got to be the banker and still ended up with all the money. The other kids liked it because they had a chance to win the game. And all the Binder kids *loved* building forts out of furniture.

"I'll play Bank," David agreed, finally lifting up his head and taking his eyes off the hardware flyer.

"Me too," said TJ.

"Fine, but next rainy day we're gonna play *Monopoly*," said Matthew.

Mom walked into the kitchen. "Did I hear someone mention playing Bank? Well, Bank cannot begin until after my talk show is over at eleven. Last time you played that game I had to watch TV on a folding chair because someone bought all the sofa cushions out from underneath of me. And just a word of warning," she added, "If you kids put one scratch on my new dining room chairs they are going to be off limits from Bank from now on. Are we clear?"

The children gave half-hearted nods and let out deep sighs. "Okay what do you all want to do until eleven?" Stephen asked.

"Tea party!" Claudia squealed. Her brothers were too polite to tell her there was no way they were going to play tea party, but not so generous that they were willing to give up their morning for it. So quietly, without making eye contact with their sister, the boys got up from the table, cleared their bowls, and hurriedly headed up to their rooms.

Chapter 4
Pencils

The kids ended up doing their own thing until their mother's favorite talk show ended. Matthew wanted a battle rematch, but Stephen was more interested in getting the Bank money organized into a toy mailbox that always served as his cash register, leaving Matthew to work on battle plans alone. David went back to work at his desk, trying to figure out a way to support the skateboard tunnel he was trying to create. Claudia had her tea party with only her stuffed animals present. TJ decided to take a better look at the pencils he found in the Uncle Harry box yesterday.

TJ was sitting at his desk when he opened the black box for the second time. The etched message on the outside still had him puzzled. *Warning: For Real Artists Only*, he read silently. What on Earth would make a bunch of black pencils so special that only a real artist could use them? he wondered as he took the lid off the box. He decided to carefully take his time and look over each pencil individually.

Yesterday, he had noticed that the pencil he touched made his fingers tingle. Today the same thing happened again, only this time the feeling was stronger, and the urge to start drawing made his fingers twitch. Nervous about what was happening, he decided to dump the pencils onto his desk.

He turned each pencil on its side, revealing the word etched into the wood. There were twelve pencils in all. The titles on the sides read: *Animals, Land, Equipment, Plants, Furniture, Food, Transportation, Clothing, Beverages, Shelter, Toys,* and *Water*. After he read the last pencil, he looked at the pile and noticed an odd, rubber, finger-shaped object. What is this thing? he wondered. Maybe it is an eraser of some sort. When he gently rubbed it across a piece of paper, very tiny, and seemingly harmless, sparks were created between the eraser and the paper. Weird. Okay, maybe not an eraser, thought TJ and he put it back in the box.

As he put the rubber finger back, he looked into the box to see if anything else was left inside. A piece of paper lay in the bottom. As he tried to pry it out, he realized the pale blue piece of paper was actually taped to the box. Gently, TJ removed it from its spot and unfolded it. Inside there was a message that read:

You must be quite talented if you were able to open this box—only someone who possesses true artistic skill can remove the lid. With the power of these pencils come certain responsibilities:

1. Never leave the lid off the box or leave the pencils unattended. The items inside should never be used by someone who is unable to remove the lid.

2. Only use the pencils when you are in a good mood. This is VERY important. The pencils respond to your thoughts and feelings.

3. Each pencil has a specific purpose. Carefully choose your pencil before you begin drawing.

4. DO NOT LOSE THE ERASER!

5. Do have fun.

Don't forget you have a special gift that very few others have. Be responsible and follow the rules.

After reading the message, TJ could not decide if he was excited or scared. It seemed as though the pencils held some kind of magic abilities. His mind immediately raced, wondering about all the things the pencils might be able to do. What if I can draw money? he thought, suddenly appreciating Stephen's love for the green paper.

Quickly though, his mind came back to reality as he realized he was hoping for too much. Luck like that just does not happen for me, he thought sadly. Then, he thought about a very simple way of testing the pencils. The blue paper said that a person must have artistic talent to be able to open the box. If this was true, and they meant a talent to draw, then David would never be able to take the lid off. David was very talented at a lot of things, but drawing was not one of them. TJ decided to test his theory. Quickly tossing all the pencils back in the box, and putting the pale blue paper and rubber finger on top of them, TJ placed the lid back on the box. Once again, just for good measure, he tried to open the box himself and for the third time, the lid came off with ease. TJ put the lid back on again, and headed over to David's desk.

David was making M-shaped supports out of pipe cleaners. TJ stood behind him, looking at a messy diagram that showed three M-shaped objects of increasing height lined up, with a tunnel resting in the V section of the M. David was almost done when he started pulling the pipe cleaners back into straight lines to try again. TJ marveled at how David could sit there and keep working on the same thing over and over and over again. Just watching was giving TJ a headache.

"What?" David asked impatiently, disrupting the thought in TJ's head.

TJ shook his head to come back to reality. "Oh, ah yeah, hmm, I was wondering ..." TJ fumbled, trying to remember why he was standing there.

"What?" David asked again. "You either want something or you don't, but whatever it is you need to quit leaning over my shoulder." He gave TJ a light shove with his elbow to push him back. "After the ants yesterday, I don't trust you." He looked back at TJ with an expression that meant he was serious.

"Yeah, man, I'm sorry about that. But you have to admit it was pretty funny? Right?" TJ joked, giving David a light push. David was in no mood for fooling around though, and TJ knew he'd better hurry up before David lost his patience. "Yeah, okay," he started again. "So, I found this box in the trash yesterday and I keep trying to get the lid off, but I can't. It seems to be stuck." He handed David the box.

In a very serious voice, David replied, "TJ, if I open this box and anything, and I mean anything jumps out at me, bites me, or can even look at me, I promise you, you will not live to tell Mom and Dad."

"Geez man, don't be so suspicious. Have some faith, would ya? Besides, think of how stupid that would be. I have no place to run and hide, not even the backyard. And I think Mom is so annoyed with me right now, she probably wouldn't stop you if you did try to hurt me."

"Yeah it would be foolish but, TJ, sometimes you specialize in foolish," David said, looking at him narrowly.

"Come on, man, could you just try and open it for me? I want to know what is inside for a real artist to see," said TJ.

David relaxed and took the box, his eyes scanning the words etched in the lid, *Warning: For Real Artists Only.*

"Well, if you are nothing else, you are a real artist," David said as he tried to pry the lid from the box. But the lid would not budge. It was as though it was stuck on with glue. "This is crazy," David said. "Are you sure this is not some kind of trick?" He eyed TJ suspiciously, as he reached for a screwdriver from his desk drawer.

TJ did not reply, amazed by the fact that his brother could not open the lid. Could there actually be something to these pencils? TJ wondered. When he noticed David about to go after the lid with a screwdriver, he jerked the box from David, and panicked, yelling, "No!"

David looked at him in confusion. "I thought you wanted to know what was in there. Wait, you *did* put something in there to try and scare me, didn't you? TJ, I swear…"

"No, no it's nothing like that, I just don't want you to ruin the box," TJ said, taking another step away from David and holding the box tight against his chest.

"I wasn't going to ruin it, just open it. What is the matter with you? Why are you so jumpy?" David asked.

"Never mind, I'll figure something out, it's okay. Thanks for trying," TJ said, heading back to his own desk. David watched his brother for another few seconds, but then turned away, shaking his head. TJ was glad to know that there was an element of magic to the box, even if it was simply getting it open. However, now he knew David was on full alert. He may have turned away, but he would be watching TJ like a hawk.

TJ had to be very careful. He was not ready to share the pencils with anyone yet. He needed to find out what happened when he actually used them before he said anything. As soon as he knew if there was any real magic to the pencils, David would be the first one he would tell, but right now he needed more time.

Sitting down at his desk again, he turned his back to his brother and hunched his shoulders for privacy. He decided to take out some of his best drawing paper, the kind he saved for school work and art projects. He laid it to one side of his desk. Then, before opening the box again, he looked toward David to make sure he was not watching. Fortunately, David was still working on his own project and seemed to be disinterested in TJ and the box.

Slowly and gently, TJ lifted the lid from the box. This time the points of the pencils seemed like glowing swirls of different colors. TJ reached in and picked one up. The word *Animals* was written on its side. Looking back at the blue piece of paper, TJ reread the responsibilities. He mentally checked off number two. He was in a great mood. Number three said to only use the pencil for the purpose listed on the side. He figured he was supposed to draw an animal with this pencil.

A tingling sensation had started in his fingers when he first picked up the pencil, and was now so strong he almost felt like he had no control over what he was about to draw. He noticed the tip of the pencil was a magnificent iridescent golden-orange. The urge to draw a school of goldfish came over him and the next thing he knew he was moving his hand across the page with such easy, purposeful strokes. First, the outlined shape of fish appeared. Then his hand worked swiftly over each individual goldfish, bringing it to life with scales, eyes, and a mouth. The shades of gold and orange adjusted as he filled in the details of each fish. It was amazing to see the pictures as he created them on the paper. They almost looked three dimensional. His hand accelerated in speed as he continued drawing. It seemed hard to believe he was actually in control of the pencil and not the other way around.

Just as he put the finishing touches on the picture, his mother walked in. "Hey guys, I just finished three loads of laundry, and I need you to come downstairs right now and pick your things out of the pile and fold them."

"In a minute Mom," TJ and David said, almost in unison.

"No, not in a minute; I want you downstairs now," Mom said. "Come on, I am not walking away from this door until I see both of you moving in my direction."

TJ knew better than to try and argue. She was right. They would procrastinate and then end up getting fussed at again. TJ hated to leave his picture behind, but was not too worried. He just had to make sure he got finished with his laundry and back upstairs before David. As he followed David out the door, TJ did not see that the fish he had drawn had just come to life.

Chapter 5
Discovery

Downstairs, the children quickly went through the pile of clothes. Claudia's things were the easiest to separate, mostly because they were made of fabrics and colors the boys didn't wear. Stephen and Matthew would have had the hardest time separating their things if they cared about to whom a pair of underpants really belonged. As twins, they had nearly identical clothing. Instead of wasting time being picky about ownership, they just threw all of their things into one big pile and divided it evenly. They each got the same number of socks, jeans, underpants, and shirts. Once the other kids had removed their belongings from the clean clothes pile, it was quick work for David and TJ.

While TJ pulled and folded his clothes from the diminishing pile, he kept thinking about his picture upstairs. How real the fish looked on the page! He wanted to look at the picture again, and run his hand over it. Once his clothes were sloppily folded, he headed upstairs. As he approached his room, he heard a strange noise coming from behind the door. It sounded like tiny thumps. He knew it could not be David because he was still downstairs carefully folding his laundry, and a few minutes behind TJ.

When TJ opened the door, his jaw dropped along with all of his clothes. Strewn across his desk, and on the floor nearby, were live goldfish exactly like the ones he had drawn just minutes ago. Without any water, the fish were struggling to stay alive, flipping back and forth on the desk and on the floor.

Quickly, TJ grabbed a beach bucket from his closet. It was filled with the buttons he'd found, as well as other ammunition he had saved for the slingshot. He dumped the contents out and raced from the bedroom to the bathroom to fill the bucket with water. On his way, he saw David heading up the stairs. Trying not to think about his brother, TJ continued to the bathroom, filled the bucket with water, and was back at the door to his bedroom. But before he could rescue the fish, he had to deal with a confused and angry David.

"Where did these fish come from? What is going on here TJ?" David demanded.

"I'll explain in a second, right now I really need help to get these fish in this bucket of water before they die," TJ said anxiously.

David's hand landed squarely on TJ's chest. "TJ, I am going to help you, but then you're going to answer some questions for me, understand?"

"Sure," TJ said.

Before David came to help pick up fish, he closed and locked their bedroom door. Together they loaded goldfish into the bucket, with TJ quietly counting them as they went in.

"How many are there?" David asked.

"Twenty," TJ said.

"Are you sure we got them all picked up? I don't want to wake in the middle of the night to the smell of old fish," David said.

For some reason TJ found this funny and started smiling, "Gross man, no, I'm sure there are twenty. Remember, I have to share this room too and I don't want to smell old fish any more than you do."

David smiled too and relaxed his shoulders, letting TJ know he was not still as angry. But TJ also knew his brother was not going to let him go before he gave him some answers. Trying to hide the pencils from David was out of the question, but TJ was not sure where to begin.

"Okay TJ, what gives? You've been acting squirrely all day? What are you hiding?" David asked.

TJ figured the very beginning was probably the best place to start. He told David about where he found the box and about the lid.

"You did not open that lid just by lifting it off?" David said.

"Yes I did," TJ said. TJ sat in his desk chair and put the *Animal* pencil back in the box and closed the lid. Then he handed the box to David again and challenged him to open it. Again, David struggled, but could not get the lid off the box. He handed it to TJ who took the lid off with ease.

David raised one eyebrow and asked, "Is this some kind of magic trick?"

TJ shook his head. "No." He showed David the piece of light blue paper and let him read it. "See, according to the first sentence the only reason I can open this box is because I have true artistic ability," TJ explained. "At first I thought it was some kind of joke, so that's why I asked you to try and open it. When you couldn't get the lid off, I realized that maybe something else was going on here."

"Okay," said David. "So where did the goldfish come from?"

"Well, I am not one hundred percent sure, but I think from the drawing I made right here," TJ said, holding up the picture drew, which now was just a flat image of the goldfish. "All I know for sure is when I picked up this pencil with the word *Animal* on it, my fingers started tingling. I thought about goldfish and drew this picture. I am not sure how they became real. Mom came and got us to go fold clothes, so I didn't see anything happen."

TJ had pulled a lot of pranks in his eleven years, but David was probably the one person who could always tell when he was truly serious. TJ looked him directly in the eyes to let him know that this was not a joke. "Okay, so why don't you try to draw something else and we can see what happens," David said. "What do you want to draw now?"

"Well I kind of think since I have all these goldfish, I should draw an aquarium for them to swim in," TJ said.

"I like it," agreed David. "I hope it works. It would be pretty cool to have an aquarium in our room. Okay, so what's next?"

"Well, just glancing at the pencils, I guess I should use the one labeled, *Furniture*? That is the closest thing I can come up with," TJ guessed.

Without touching any of the pencils, David looked at the different labels on the sides and agreed. "I don't really see anything else that would fit except maybe *Equipment*. Yeah, try the *Furniture* one first and let's see what happens."

David dragged his desk chair over by TJ, while TJ got out the large pad of paper again. TJ took a deep breath, then, very carefully, he picked up the pencil. Immediately, his fingers tingled and the pencil tip glowed. In his mind,

TJ could see the aquarium as clearly as he could see his hand. Suddenly and swiftly, his hand moved across the page. David sat close by, watching.

Again, TJ's body was transformed into a trance-like state. The silver color flew from the tip of the pencil and created the shiny image of the sides of the aquarium. TJ knew his hand was moving. He could feel his right hand, yet somehow felt as if he had no control over what it was doing. The pencil tip went from silver to translucent. TJ could hear a sound, like the squeaking of someone cleaning glass, as he drew the sides of the fish tank. The speed of his hand got faster and faster as he put the finishing touches on the picture. TJ had never felt so intensely focused on anything before in his life.

Within a few minutes, a picture of a rectangular aquarium shone back from the paper. The picture had a three dimensional look, as if it was somehow coming off the paper. Both boys were unsure what to do next or what to expect.

Then suddenly, VOOSH!

The aquarium popped off the page and sat in the center of TJ's desk. The boys jumped up with their eyes wide open. David was the first to speak. "Awesome!"

TJ grinned from ear to ear. He could feel the inside of his chest swelling with excitement and pride. "Wow," he whispered. "You dream of stuff like this happening."

"Yeah," David mumbled.

The implications of what just happened were so enormous that neither one of them knew what to say next. They stood side by side, turning their heads back and forth, looking at the aquarium then looking at each other. Finally, it was TJ who spoke. "I guess we should get some water and fill this thing up, huh?"

"Yeah, I mean, no," said David, shaking his head.

TJ was puzzled. He thought maybe David was concerned about how they would explain their new aquarium and fish to their parents. "It's okay, we can just say a kid at school came by and asked us to watch it while his family was on vacation this summer. Mom and Dad won't suspect a thing."

"No, that's not what I mean," said David. "I mean that is a good idea, and ... you came up with that story so fast it's a good thing you're so uncomfortable about lying to an adult. But I was talking about the water. Didn't you say one of the pencils had the word *Water* on the side? Why do we have to go get water? Can't you just draw the water and make that appear too?"

"Yes," said TJ slowly, surprised at himself for not thinking of it first. "Yes, I can. I can draw water. Man this is going to be so cool." He and David lifted up the aquarium and moved it to one side of the desk, revealing the picture of the aquarium on the paper. Then both boys sat down as TJ put the *Furniture* pencil in the black box and picked up the pencil marked *Water*. "I guess I just draw the water right in the picture with the aquarium, huh?" he asked, looking at David.

"Sounds good to me. Give it a try and let's see what happens."

TJ's fingers tingled and his hand moved again. All the while, the tip of the pencil glowed and emitted a pale blue color. The way TJ's hand moved across the page resembled that of a concert pianist's playing a complicated symphony. Within minutes, the water had been sketched in the picture of the aquarium, and started to take on the same three dimensional appearance of the other drawings. This time the boys were ready and braced themselves for the water to become a reality.

WHOOSH!

SPLASH!

Suddenly, the fish tank was filled with water. "This is beyond cool," David said, staring in awe at the aquarium. TJ shook his head in amazement. Then, without saying a word, he reached for a different pencil, the one marked *Plants*. As if David was reading his mind, he said, "Good idea! This is going to be the most awesome aquarium ever!"

TJ's hand went to work again, quickly drawing small plants into the picture of the aquarium still on his desk. While TJ worked his magic with the pencil, David went to get the bucket of fish. After the picture was done and the plants had magically transported themselves from the paper to the fish tank, the two boys carefully put the fish into their new home.

Together they lifted the heavy tank and placed it on top of the dresser located between their beds. After some readjustments to make sure it was in the perfect spot, David and TJ sat down on their beds and admired the scene. "I hope Mom and Dad don't get too upset about this thing. You know how Mom keeps reminding us we cannot have any pets," David said.

"Nah, I'm not worried about it, these are just goldfish," TJ said. "She doesn't have to cook for them or bathe them or anything like that. I'm more curious to see how long it takes one of them to notice that we even have a fish tank."

"Well, let's hope it is no time soon, and that Mom buys your excuse," David said with one eyebrow raised. Then, changing the subject, he asked, "Hey, what time is it?"

"Five minutes after eleven, why?" TJ asked.

"Because we are supposed to be downstairs getting ready to play Bank. We better get moving before Stephen steals our money, or Claudia and Matthew buy everything," he said.

"Geez, I almost forgot about that," TJ said, standing up. "We can't leave Stephen alone with the money too long. He cheats every time we play Bank. If I didn't actually like the part where we build forts, then I would have quit playing this game a long time ago."

"Yeah, me too," agreed David as he got up. Then suddenly he stopped. "Hey wait a minute. I just got a great idea!"

When TJ turned to look at his brother, he was wearing a devious smile that let TJ know instantly he was going to like the idea, whatever it was. David did not often plot and scheme, but when he did, it was always good. "Alright, you have my attention," said TJ. "What's running through that head of yours?"

"Oh, I think you're gonna love this one. It will make Stephen crazy," David said, putting his arms over TJ's shoulders and whispering in his ear.

TJ listened, slowly forming a smirk that matched his brother's. When David was done, TJ said, "That plan is perfect. I gotta admit, sometimes I like the way you think!"

Chapter 6
Bank

As the two older boys were heading down the stairs, they ran into their mother with her raincoat on. "I was just coming to find you two," she said.

"Where are you going?" TJ asked.

"Oh, Ms. Watkins is hosting a bridge game and one of the ladies got sick, so they need someone to fill in as a fourth player. I told her I could come over. Now, I expect all of you to be on your best behavior. I have already talked to the others and told them you were in charge," she said, looking at David. "David, as the oldest, I want you to keep an eye on things, but if there is a problem you call me. And no fighting! Do you hear me?" She paused, giving them both a hard stare. "I mean it. I especially expect you two older boys to behave yourselves and get along."

David put an arm around TJ's neck and squeezed, joking, "Aw, come on Mom, do I look like I would hurt this guy? I just love him soooo much." He pulled TJ in even tighter and gave him a big kiss on the cheek.

"Yeah, I can feel the love" she said. "Now listen, you two set a good example and behave and take care of the others. I am only a few houses away and I should be back shortly. I love you." Then she put her hands on the sides of each boy's face and kissed him on the forehead. "Behave," was her final word before she went downstairs, pulling her raincoat hood over her head, and walked out the door.

"Man, the timing is perfect," David said, grinning at TJ.

They found the other kids sitting in the den, staring over the pile of money Stephen had neatly sorted. As the banker, Stephen gave each child one fifth of the money. Once it was evenly distributed, each child stored their money in a safe place. David kept his in a wallet that he could chain to his belt loops, TJ kept his in an old cigar box, Matthew stored his in one of his father's old tool boxes, and Claudia held her money tightly against her side in a small, white patent leather pocketbook she had gotten for Easter two years back. Stephen continued to use the highly coveted mailbox since he would get most of the money back as the children "bought" furniture from around the house.

Although each child had a unique place to keep their money safe, the money never stayed in their possession very long. Stephen distributed approximately six thousand dollars in fake money to each sibling. Once everyone had their money, Stephen announced the beginning of the game. The den quickly turned into a scene that resembled the floor of the New York Stock Exchange, with each child madly waving money in the air and screaming out the items they wanted to buy before anyone else could get to them.

Before anyone had a chance to think, Claudia quickly called out, "I want the den sofa for five thousand dollars."

Matthew started talking before Claudia finished. "I want the kitchen table and chairs for four thousand, one of Dad's bungee cords for five hundred, and two dining room tablecloths for another thousand."

Around this time, at least one argument usually broke out because someone wanted something that someone else had, but today there was silence.

Stephen looked over at TJ and David who had not said a word. "Okay, Claudia and Matthew, your purchases are granted. Pay up," Stephen said.

"Are you buying anything today, Stephen?" TJ asked.

The question was unexpected. "Uh, sure, but you guys know I always wait until the very end to buy anything," Stephen replied.

"Right, so you can get if for a discount, like a clearance item," said TJ.

Stephen's cheeks reddened with embarrassment. "Well, if no one else wants something and I am stuck with the leftovers, then I should get a break on the price."

By this time, Claudia and Matthew had already started working on their forts. Claudia pulled all the cushions off the sofa and stacked them together, creating a perfect-sized hideout for a seven-year-old girl and a group of her stuffed animals. Matthew had already gotten the bungee cord from the garage and was in the process of stacking chairs upside down on the kitchen table when Stephen nervously glanced his way.

TJ and David stared at their brother. "So then I guess you expect us to buy the living room or dining room and pay full price right now?" TJ asked.

"Sure, whichever you want. I don't mind taking the leftovers," said Stephen.

"What if I said all I want is one dining room tablecloth?" TJ asked.

"Fine, but how are you going to make a fort out of that? You will lose the contest," said Stephen.

"I'll take my chances. One tablecloth, please. Five hundred dollars, right?" said TJ, handing the money to Stephen.

"You know you can't use any furniture in your fort if you don't buy it from the bank. Those are the rules," Stephen said, clearly frustrated that TJ was not spending more money.

"We know," said David. "All I want to buy is one tablecloth as well."

"Even if you use poles from the garage, you have to pay for them. Those are the Bank rules," said Stephen.

Matthew had already used the bungee cord to hold together the legs of the chairs that were stacked upside down on the table. He then put his large tablecloth over the whole contraption, creating a fort that looked quite tall and impressive. "You two will never build something larger or stronger than this," he said.

"Yeah, you are going to have to buy some big furniture if you think you are going to beat Matthew," Stephen said as TJ and David walked away.

Heading up the stairs, TJ had a hard time containing himself. He loved the fact that Stephen had no idea what they were up to. He was pretty sure Stephen would forgive both he and David once they saw their fort.

"We don't have a lot of time," said David. "Stephen, Matthew, and Claudia will be snooping around here in a few minutes wondering what we are up to."

TJ had already laid the large white tablecloth on the floor. "I will get started right away. I already have a great visual in my head. I just need to pick out the right pencil."

He took out a clean sheet of paper and looked in the pencil box. As soon as he found the *Food* pencil, he began drawing. Like all the previous times, he had an image in his head of what he wanted to draw. The pencil tip started off with a swirl of brown colors. He first outlined the image on the paper. As he continued to draw, he filled in all the spaces. After all the brown parts were colored in, the tip quickly changed to red, than green, then white, and continued changing through almost every color of the rainbow. The longer his hand was moving, the deeper his trance-like state became.

When he finally finished the picture, he was exhausted and very hungry. He wondered if the hunger had anything to do with the fact that he had just used the *Food* pencil.

David watched as TJ drew. Once TJ was done, the boys sat eagerly awaiting for the image to come to life.

VOOSH!

Just like the previous times, the picture popped off the page and landed in the middle of the room. This time there was a thud as the enormous structure hit the floor.

"WOW!" said TJ and David together. The fort was even better than they had imagined.

Outside the bedroom door, TJ heard the sound of footsteps and whispering. He knew his siblings would be wondering what he and David were doing. "Hey David, quick, help me get this other tablecloth over this thing. I don't want them to see it until we are ready."

The boys covered the fort then opened the door. Standing right outside were Stephen, Matthew, and Claudia.

"Hey, I was just coming to look for you guys," TJ said with a smile.

"We heard a loud thud. Are you okay?" asked Claudia.

"We are better than okay, little sis. We are fantastic! Come in and close the door."

Together they walked into the bedroom just a few steps behind TJ. All they saw was something that looked like a large bumpy object covered by one of the tablecloths. It was sitting in the middle of the floor on top of the other tablecloth which had been spread out like a picnic blanket.

"On the count of three, prepare to be amazed," David said.

"It looks like a tablecloth fort without a door," Stephen said, critically. "And, if there is any furniture under there, you are going to owe the bank some money, with interest."

TJ could tell he was still aggravated that he and David never bought anything.

"I guarantee you that there is no furniture under this tablecloth, Stephen. I also guarantee you that this tablecloth is covering a fort that will go down in the Binder family history as the most awesome fort ever," bragged TJ. He stuck out his chest and held his chin higher.

The others remained silent as David and TJ counted, lifting the tablecloth, "One ... two ... three!"

Together they carefully flipped the covering off the structure, revealing a gigantic, kid-sized, gingerbread house. It was the most delicious-looking fort ever! The children's eye popped. The fort was bigger than Claudia's, but the whole thing was edible! The roof and the walls were made of gingerbread generously covered with icing. The front door and shutters were gigantic rectangles of sugar cookies with sugar sprinkles that sparkled in the light. The chimney was made out of cubes of hard red candies. The whole structure was decorated with gumdrops, chocolate, licorice, and other assorted candies and treats.

It took a few minutes for anyone to say anything, but then everyone spoke at once.

"Awesome!" said Stephen, forgetting all about the money.

"Wow!" exclaimed Matthew.

"Yummy!" squealed Claudia. "When can we start eating it?"

"Yeah," asked Matthew, "Can we eat it?"

TJ beamed with pride, but David was stunned. "Don't you guys even want to know how we made it?"

"No, I don't care. It looks so delicious; I want to eat it!" said Claudia enthusiastically. "I want to start with the roof and walls with candy decorations, and keep chewing until I get to the sugar cookie on the front door!" Claudia's sweet tooth was legendary in the Binder family. Once, during 'The Binder Family Cake Eating Contest' she beat all the boys.

"Hold on. Stephen and Matthew, aren't either of you curious how we baked and built this whole fort so quick?" David asked, incredulously.

"And without ever going into the kitchen," TJ added.

Suddenly, even Claudia stopped thinking about eating and starting thinking about what their brothers had just said. "It is a little odd that you magically had all this food up here," Matthew said.

"Exactly!" David replied, hardly able to contain his excitement. "Magic is the key word! You are not going to believe what TJ found!"

"Wait," interrupted Claudia, whose sweet tooth was back in control again, "Can we taste something before you tell us how this happened? I am drooling on myself."

"Sure," TJ said. "But once you have something to eat, sit down so we can show you the biggest miracle that ever happened to the Binder family."

The younger children charged at the fort and started taking pieces off it and shoveling them into their mouths. Everything tasted just as delicious as it looked. The gingerbread walls tasted as if they had just come out of the oven. The icing was the sweetest and richest buttercream icing the children ever savored. David and TJ also started devouring parts of the enormous treat. TJ was thrilled at how yummy the fort tasted.

After a few minutes of gorging on sweets, the children sat on the floor and listened as David and TJ explained about the magic pencils. TJ finished by holding up the paper with the identical image of the fort. "What you see before you started out as this," he said.

The other children seemed skeptical at first, rolling their eyes and saying things like, "Yeah, right, Mr. Magician."

But then David pointed out the fish tank. "Explain how we got this then?" he challenged.

"Some kid in the neighborhood asked you to watch it while they were on vacation," Stephen suggested.

David and TJ laughed. TJ realized he'd have to demonstrate with the pencils before he was believed. So, he called his siblings over to the desk. He took the picture of the aquarium, again pointing out that it was identical to the real one sitting on their dresser. Using the *Animal* pencil, he decided to add some fish to the tank. He wanted to draw something other than goldfish, so his siblings would notice the new fish when they appeared in the tank. He decided on guppies.

Stephen, Matthew, and Claudia stood looking over TJ's shoulder as he drew. They saw the way the tip of the pencil swirled with color and how, without pencils being changed, the color on the page adapted as needed. They also noted how TJ appeared to be in some sort of trance as he drew.

TJ had just finished sketching the fish and started to lift the pencil from the paper, when the fish took on a three-dimensional appearance. Then suddenly, SPLASH! The fish appeared in the tank.

"Wow!" they all shouted in unison. But before they could get too excited, the fun came to a crashing halt.

The sound of the front door opening rang through the house, followed by, "Hello kiddos, I'm home!"

"Mom!" Claudia said with her eyes wide.

"I thought she was going to be gone longer," TJ whispered.

"Well too late, she's here now. What are we going to do with this fort?" David asked.

"Can we hide it in the closet?" suggested Matthew

"Just put the tablecloth back over it, maybe she won't notice it," Stephen said.

"What is that rubber finger thingy?" Claudia asked, pointing in the black box. "Is that an eraser? Can you erase the picture and make the fort disappear?"

TJ looked at Claudia, surprised. "The rubber finger thingy? Why didn't I think of that?" TJ wondered out loud.

"Yeah, see what the rubber finger can do TJ," David said.

TJ grabbed the rubber finger from the black box and pushed it across the page, over the drawing of the edible fort. Sparks flew as he moved it from side to side, and back and forth. Miraculously, as he pressed it over the picture, both the image on the paper and the fort in the middle of the floor started to disappear.

"It is awful quiet up there. What are you all doing?" Mom asked, her voice getting closer and closer to the room.

"Hurry, TJ! She's coming," the others whispered.

TJ was just about done when the door to the room opened. "Hey, what are you doing in here? I thought you were playing Bank," she said suspiciously.

"We were going to, but TJ started showing us some magic tricks first," Matthew sort of lied.

"Magic tricks? I thought I very clearly told you those were off-limits after the incident with the Buras boy! That poor child spent three days in the hospital when one of you tried to 'magically' saw him in half."

"It was nothing like that, Mom. This was just a card trick where TJ tries to guess which card I am holding," said Stephen. "He's really not very good. TJ, you need to practice more before making us all come up here, wasting our time."

"Well, since you are not playing Bank, I would like these two tablecloths put back in the dining room, and any cushions or chairs put back where they belong," said Mom. "I am going to start on dinner. I'm making your grandmother's shrimp creole recipe. Claudia, do you mind helping me set the table?"

"Sure!" said Claudia. "Can I put out the pretty green tablecloth, the one Grandma loved, since we are having her favorite?"

"I think that would be a nice tribute to Grandma," Mom replied. Then she turned to walk out of the room. "Hey, is that the Adams' fish tank? I know Tim wanted us to watch it while they were on vacation. I'm glad he remembered to bring it over."

After she left, the children breathed sighs of relief.

"That was close," TJ said. "I'm putting these things away for now. Maybe I will bring them when we go out to play tomorrow, and we can try some new things with them. For now, we all need to stay out of trouble, so we don't get grounded."

"Agreed," said David.

"One hundred percent!" said Claudia.

Chapter 7
Claudia

TJ clearly remembered the day his parents brought Claudia home from the hospital. He was only four years old, but he remembered seeing her swaddled in a tiny pink blanket with only her face showing her gentle little features. She seemed so fragile. He'd vowed at that moment to always look out for her and protect her like a big brother should.

As the years passed and she grew bigger and stronger, TJ realized that she was not as delicate as he'd originally thought. In fact, compared to most girls that he knew, she was pretty tough. That did not change the way he felt about her though. Along with his brothers, he made sure everyone at River Springs Elementary knew that if you messed with Claudia, you were going to face the Binder brothers. The boys included her in whatever they were doing, and always took her with them when they went outside and headed beyond the neighborhood on adventures. In return, Claudia was completely loyal to her brothers.

The only time of day Claudia wished she had a sister was at night. She had a terrible fear of the dark and never wanted to be alone. She was always worried that something would come out from under her bed and get her.

"Let's get a dog," TJ suggested one day, when Claudia was complaining about having to go to bed. "Then we can have an extra playmate, and Claudia can have a roommate at night."

Once Claudia heard TJ's idea, she started asking her parents for a dog every night before bed. Her dad was not completely opposed, but her mother would not hear of it. "I do not need one more living thing to take care of," she said.

TJ felt sorry for his sister, but knew his mother would never change her mind. So that night, following his discovery of the magic pencils, TJ decided to do something nice for Claudia. She will love this, he thought.

He tiptoed into her room, where she lay sleeping, and eased into the oversized chair in the corner. He could see the top of her strawberry blonde head poking out from underneath the covers.

He took out the pad of large white paper and removed the pencil labeled *Animals* from the black box. Immediately his fingers began to tingle and twitch. In his mind he could see what he was going to draw as clearly as if it was sitting in front of him. His fingers moved quickly and nimbly across the page, creating the image he had in his mind. It was just like the note said; the pencils could read his thoughts. As he sketched, the lines flew from his fingers through the pencil. The tip glowed, emitting a warm, coffee-brown color. At first, the strokes of brown looked like a messy pile of chocolate spaghetti. But faster than the eye could keep up, the shape of the object became clearer. The fur on the legs and tail took shape. The body and head began to look incredibly life-like. Once he had put the finishing touches on the ears and nose, the brown dog popped off the page and came to life, leaving only a flat copy of the image on the paper.

Feeling his legs for the first time, the dog raced in circles, chasing his tail. He let out a *rrowf*!

TJ tossed aside the pencil and paper, and jumped over to hold the dog, to keep him from barking again. Unfortunately, it was too late. That one bark had gotten the attention of Claudia, who sat up in bed and rubbed her eyes. When she stopped rubbing and looked over the end of her bed to the floor, she seemed unable to believe what she saw. She rubbed them again just to be sure she wasn't imagining things. A dog, a real live dog, was in her bedroom running in circles and rolling on the floor. Then she saw TJ. "Oh Thomas Joseph, he's beautiful! Where did you find him? How did you get him up here? Did Mom and Dad say it was okay?" She sounded anxious as she spoke the final question.

"Shhhh," TJ said, putting a finger to his lips and hoping his parents did not hear the dog yelp. "He is a special present just for you, but you can only keep him at night. And no, Mom and Dad have no idea and if they find out

I'm going to be in really big trouble, so you can't say a word to anyone. Okay?"

"What about the boys; do they know?" Claudia asked, as she climbed out of the bed and got down on the floor with the dog, rubbing his belly.

"No, nobody knows. I just made him," TJ said.

"With the magic pencils?" Claudia asked.

"Yes, but in the morning I am going to have to erase him. But don't worry, I will draw him again every night for you," TJ assured her.

"Oh Thomas Joseph, you are the best brother in the whole wide world!" she exclaimed, jumping up and giving him a big hug.

"Well, I just don't want you to grow up and hate all of us." TJ looked across the room at the still-bandaged Cuddles.

"Hate you guys? I would never hate you guys! I have the best brothers in the world!" she said softly.

"Even though we beat up your stuffed animals and get you in trouble with us?" TJ asked, puzzled.

Claudia looked confused. "You do realize stuffed animals cannot really feel anything, don't you?"

"Well yeah," said TJ. "But I know you love those things."

"Yeah, well what I love was when Bert Loft tried to make me give him my ice cream money. All of you circled him and told him you would crush him like a tin can," she said, smiling. "And the time I fell off my bike over by the McAllister's farm? David gave me a piggy-back ride the whole way home, while you and Stephen carried my bike. And ..." she said with a dramatic pause, "what about you just making me a dog?" she squealed enthusiastically. "Which I love waaaaaayyy better than any stuffed animal, even if I can only keep him at night."

"Okay, but if you ever think you might be starting to hate us, please let me know," he said, giving her arm a gentle squeeze.

"Never gonna happen," Claudia said, smiling. She climbed back up on her bed and patted the covers to let the dog know it was okay to join her. Without hesitating, it hopped on the bed and curled next to Claudia. As she laid her head down, she put one arm over the dog, cuddling next to him.

TJ leaned over to tuck her in and asked, "Hey, have you thought about what you are going to call him?"

Claudia's eyes lit up as she pulled the dog in tight and, without hesitating, whispered, "Magic."

"That's perfect," said TJ, smiling, proud of what he had done. Then he turned to pick up his pad and pencils, and took one look back before leaving the room. Claudia was already asleep. If my parents could see this, they would absolutely let her have a dog, he thought, as he pulled the door closed behind him.

Chapter 8
Fort

The next morning, TJ woke extra early, worried that his parents would find the dog. He hopped out of bed and went to his dresser to erase the dog from the page. Only this time, when he moved the rubber finger across the page, it did not make any sparks. Curious, he took the eraser and the picture and went into Claudia's room. Claudia and Magic were curled sound asleep on the double bed.

TJ tried the eraser again. This time, with the dog in sight, the sparks started as soon as he pushed the rubber finger over the picture. Within just a few minutes both the dog and the drawing had disappeared. That's interesting, he thought. The eraser only works when I can see the object I drew.

TJ walked back to his room, put the eraser in the black box, and closed the lid on the pencils. He laid the freshly erased paper on the top of his desk and headed downstairs.

David was sitting at the kitchen table eating pancakes with Stephen. With alarm clocks in their stomachs, they were usually the first to get up and eat breakfast.

"Would you like blueberry or plain pancakes, TJ?" Mom asked from the stove.

"Four plain ones please," TJ said, sitting down next to Stephen.

"You don't know what you're missing always eating the plain ones," Stephen said, exposing a purple mouth full of blueberry. "These are delicious! Mom, can I have four more blueberry pancakes, please?"

"Sure, as soon as I finish the plain ones for TJ," said Mom.

Outside, the sun was shining brightly again, and soon Matthew and Claudia came joined the others. Once everyone was gathered at the table, they quickly decided to head out to the "playground,"—this was code for the abandoned field where they were building their skateboard ramp—and see what was left to do. They were hoping to try out the skateboards and the ramp.

They made their plans through mouthfuls of pancakes, but with their mother standing so close they had to be careful. They did not want to give away too much information for fear that she might figure out what they were up to and put a stop to the new ramp. It was decided that David would scrounge around for tools, hardware, and anything else that might be useful for their project. Stephen, Matthew, and TJ were supposed to rummage through toy boxes, closets, and the garage for knee pads, helmets, and elbow pads. Claudia was to fill her backpack with drinks and snacks, so they could stay out almost all day.

Claudia had been unusually quiet during breakfast. "You okay kid?" David asked.

TJ knew immediately what had her upset, but did not want to have a discussion about the dog in front of anyone else. Claudia looked over at TJ, who shook his head. This was not the time or the place. So she softly whispered, "No" and got up from the table.

Once they were all dressed and outside, making their way through the neighborhood, Claudia asked, "Did I have a really weird dream last night, or did you draw me a dog with some magic pencils, Thomas Joseph?"

TJ smiled gently. "The pencils are real and so was the dog. I was afraid you would miss him this morning. Don't worry though, I saved the paper I drew him on, and plan to draw him again exactly the same tonight."

"You promise? Because I had the best sleep ever, and when I woke up this morning and Magic was gone, I was so sad. I know I just got him, but I really, really love him already, TJ."

TJ knew she must mean it because, unlike his parents, Claudia only called him TJ when she was being very serious. His mother was the exact opposite; she only called him Thomas Joseph when he was in BIG trouble. "I promise, Claudia, I will make sure Magic is there for you every night." Hoping she felt reassured, he looked over at his little sister who seemed to have cheered up, and decided to let her in on a secret. "Hey, look what I remembered," he said opening his backpack and revealing the black box.

"What will you draw with them?" Claudia asked.

"Hey, you remembered to bring the pencils with you?" asked Matthew, overhearing.

This question was enough to gain the attention of David and Stephen, and soon all the children were walking slower, huddled around TJ. "Yeah, I was thinking maybe I could draw a tree house or an outside fort for us to hang out in," TJ replied.

"What a great idea, Thomas Joseph! Can you also draw some furniture too?" Claudia asked.

"Yeah, you could draw us an awesome tree fort that is up so high no one can mess with it while we're gone," Stephen added.

"Or he could draw us a mini-castle in the middle of the woods and make a moat and a fire-breathing dragon to protect it from enemies," Matthew chimed in.

"I like the part about the dragon," TJ said, fantasizing about owning a gigantic ferocious pet that he could command. "Let's start with a fort and see what we want to draw after we have a place to hang out."

"I vote for a castle-like fort," said Claudia, agreeing with Matthew's suggestion.

"I like Stephen's idea of a tree house fort that is up high and no one else can get to," said David.

"How about I combine both ideas, building a fort that looks like a castle, but is up high in the trees where no one will notice it," TJ suggested.

"Yes!" the children agreed together. As they headed for the woods, they walked past the skateboard ramp they had been working on for the last two weeks. David walked about ten feet to the right of the ramp to be sure the skateboards were still in place. The boards were in a slight hole in the ground, hidden by grass and twigs the kids had placed on top of them. Everything was just as they had left it.

"You know we could scrap this whole thing and have TJ build us a brand new, state-of-the-art ramp," Stephen suggested.

"No way," said David. "I love the pencils and I can't wait to have TJ build us a fort, but we've put a lot of work into this ramp. I want to finish it the old-fashioned way, by building it with our own hands."

"Agreed," said TJ. "This ramp shows what we can do when we work together as a team. Let's get the treehouse fort done, so we have a place to hang out and put all our things. Then later today or tomorrow we can come back here and finish what we started."

Stephen agreed, "You're both right. We did work hard on this project. Let's finish it together."

The kids stood in the middle of the uneven field. There were woods in front, as well as to the right and the left of them. "Okay, first we need to look for a clump of trees sturdy and strong enough to hold a fort made of stone," said TJ. "Let's break into two teams. We are searching for a group of at least four or five trees together, with wide trunks and strong limbs."

David and Stephen headed towards the woods on the left side of the field. TJ, Claudia, and Matthew moved towards the woods to the right. "Hey, hold on a second," said TJ. Quickly, he got out his art pad and opened the pencil box, taking out the *Equipment* pencil. He sat in the field and began to draw. Each time he used the pencils, the speed and gracefulness of his movements improved. Less than a minute later, a picture of a pair of walkie-talkies appeared and popped off the page.

"Great idea!" said David.

"If you think you've found a set of trees that will work, let us know," said TJ, handing one walkie-talkie to David.

"We can use these all summer, even when we're in the house," said Matthew, taking a walkie-talkie out of TJ's hand and trying it out.

TJ smiled proudly, feeling important. He had the power to make things his siblings liked! He looked forward to finding a great spot for a tree house, and creating a hide-a-way they could use all year long.

The kids had only been searching the woods for about five minutes when David's voice came over the walkie-talkie. "Head back to the field and meet us there. We found the perfect trees for our fort."

TJ, Claudia, and Matthew did a quick about-face and headed back to the field. It was not long before David and Stephen came from the other direction, waving them over.

Once they were together, David led the way toward a group of seven trees. There was one tree in the center, and six trees surrounding it, as though they had been purposely planted that way. Each tree trunk was about three feet in diameter, strong and sturdy enough to carry the load TJ was planning to build. In addition, each tree had strong limbs that could support the weight of the floor and the walls.

"Great job, guys! These trees look like they were planted just for us," said TJ. "Before I start to draw, let's talk about things. We want a fort made out of stone, right?"

"Yes," the others said together.

"Do we want a lookout tower?" TJ asked.

"Yes! Make the tower round on top," Matthew said. "Hey, could you also put windows in the fort, maybe five of them, one for each kid to look out? That way we can all keep guard and see what is coming."

"Great idea, gives us a view of the woods," said TJ. "Any other ideas?"

"Could you make stairs to go up, but also put in a slide to go down?" asked Claudia.

"Hmmm," said TJ. "I think I can make that happen. It would be fun to slide down, wouldn't it?"

"Yes!" said Claudia enthusiastically.

"David or Stephen, any requests?" TJ asked.

"Can you build some kind of vault or safe where we can hide our valuables?" asked Stephen.

"Good idea. I could hide the pencils in there," said TJ. "David, how about you; do you want me to add anything?"

David smiled. "I don't think I can imagine anything as awesome as what you'll draw. I'm ready to see the fort finished."

"I hope you're right," TJ said. His fingers started tingling as soon as he touched the box. He clutched it to his chest and closed his eyes. In his mind, he could clearly visualize how the tree fort would look. A staircase would wrap around a tree trunk from the ground to about twelve feet in the air. The sides of the staircase would be high to conceal anyone using them. There would be a hidden lever at the top of the staircase and one at the bottom. The levers would be used to flatten out the stairs, so invaders could not climb up, and so the kids could slide down when leaving. At the top, the staircase would lead to a sturdy wooden door.

The entire structure would be made of grey stone, similar to the kind used to build medieval castles. The fort would extend to each of the surrounding trees, making it about fifteen feet on each side. It would be square with five windows. Each window would have shutters on the inside that could be closed and locked, to keep out rain or protect from an enemy attack. Inside the fort, there would be a staircase of stone built into the wall and leading to a sliding door for access to the roof.

Just like Matthew suggested, there would be a round lookout tower. Its walls would be high enough to protect anyone from falling off, but low enough to allow the kids to see over.

The thoughts and images flooded TJ's mind. He took a deep breath then reached into his backpack to get his pad of paper. He sat down on the ground where he could see all seven trees. As he took the lid off the box, a single pencil practically jumped into his hand. He turned it to the side to read the word *Structures*. It was the perfect pencil for the job.

"Okay, guys, I can feel the pencil starting to take over," TJ said. "Everyone stand behind me. I am not sure how this will come off the page, and I don't want anyone to get hurt."

The children moved behind TJ, and looked over his shoulder as he began to draw. The pencil tip swirled. At first, the image on the page looked like a blueprint from an architect. Dimensions and foundational details of the fort were drawn around seven trees. The image showed how the structure would be supported by the limbs and the trunks.

The pencil tip turned grey and stone walls began to appear, covering up the blue lines. The staircase wrapped around a tree trunk, just as TJ had envisioned. TJ's hand moved up the page, drawing the main part of the fort, and then to the top, creating a roof tower.

After the grey fort was drawn, the pencil tip swirled a charcoal color and TJ's hand flew up and down, and side to side, etching in shadows and shading. The image began to have the same three dimensional look that the other pictures had before they popped off the paper.

"Stand back," David said, stretching his arms in front of his siblings. As he spoke, rumbling vibrations shook the ground. A magnificent stone structure emerged out of the ground and built itself up in the cluster of trees.

TJ's hand stopped moving. He remained seated and motionless. The only thing moving were his eyes, as he followed the progress of the magic unfolding in front of him. He could not believe it. The fort was super awesome—better even than what he'd imagined.

It took about a full minute for the entire structure to appear and for the rumbling to stop. Leaves whispered and birds sang again.

"Aaaaaahhhhhhhh!" Claudia squealed.

"Holy smokes," said David breathlessly, ruffling his own hair so it stood on end as if he'd been electrocuted.

"Man, man, man," muttered Stephen, pacing to and fro in amazement. "This is sick!"

TJ stood up, and his brothers tackled him in a group hug, thumping his back. "Way to go, dude! You're the best!" Then everyone rushed to the new fort while TJ followed, grinning and dazed. The stairs were in the up position.

"Let us in!" Claudia crowed.

TJ thought back to the design and remembered drawing the hidden lever at the bottom. Reaching down, he pulled on one of the stones near the ground. It flipped up, revealing the lever.

"Don't anyone climb the stairs yet. I want to see what this will do," TJ said, as he flipped the switch into the down position. At once all the steps disappeared into the staircase and the whole thing turned into a smooth surface like a large slide.

"Mega cool," said David. He crouched next to TJ to look at the secret lever. "Flip it back up and see what happens."

TJ did and the stairs popped back up.

"Can you leave them up? I want to check this thing out," said Matthew.

TJ nodded. There was so much to take in. He wanted to study the details of every square inch of the fort. The other children clambered up the stairs and headed inside. TJ took a few extra minutes outside the fort, examining the way the walls wove through the tree branches. The fort was camouflaged by the branches and leaves. If you were standing directly under it, you would not realize it was above you, unless you were really looking for it.

TJ stepped back to look at the fort from the woods. The stairs were the only noticeable signs of the fort's existence. TJ took out his *Plants* pencil and grabbed his pad of paper. He added vines and leaves to the sides of the staircase. When the vines popped off the page and onto the fort, it was amazing. Suddenly, the fort was completely camouflaged in the forest. An unknowing stranger could easily walk right past and never see it.

Satisfied, TJ heard the others laughing upstairs, and raced to meet them.

When he walked through the door, David and Matthew were opening and closing the shutters on the windows. Stephen and Claudia were carefully inspecting the stone walls.

"You can see for miles from here," said Matthew.

TJ looked out one window. Beyond it the woods seemed to stretch forever. In front of him, level with the bottom of the window, there was a ledge. "This must be where you prop up your weapons, in case you need to fire at the enemy," said TJ.

"Hey TJ, since Mom won't buy us any toy guns, maybe you can draw some that we can leave on the shelves?" Matthew suggested.

Before TJ could respond, Claudia spoke up. "TJ, look at how cool this thing is." His sister was speaking from the middle of the wall, on a set of steps that went up to the ceiling. Her feet were planted on a protruding stone while her hands were locked on to metal rings that bordered each step, starting at the sixth stone. TJ counted twelve steps that led to the ceiling. A metal handle was attached to the ceiling above the last step. TJ remembered from the drawing that this was where the sliding door to the roof was located.

"Get down from there for a second, Claudia, and I'll show you something else," TJ said.

Once Claudia was off the stairs, TJ climbed them. When he got to the top, he pulled on the handle, and a rectangular panel popped open. It was attached by sliding metal hinges. TJ pulled the handle away from the wall and toward the center of the room. The panel slid easily out of the way. TJ continued climbing upward and out onto the roof of the fort. "Come on!" he called to the room below.

The others scrambled up the stairs and onto the rooftop lookout tower.

"This is so awesome," said David.

"I think I can see the empty lot from here," said Stephen.

"I think you're right," said Matthew.

"It's hard for me to see anything," said Claudia, who could just barely look over the stone edge.

"Sorry about that, Claudia," said TJ. "I didn't want to make it too low because I didn't want anyone to fall off. It is a long way down."

"That's okay," said Claudia. "Hey, can you draw us a sofa and a table and chairs so we have someplace to sit and play?"

"Absolutely," said TJ. "I'll come back down with you, and you can tell me what you want."

Claudia said, "Let's start with a comfy sofa that will fit in the whole corner of the room. Make it big enough for all of us to sit on at once."

"Okay," TJ said. "Any particular color?"

"I guess brown, so it won't show too much dirt."

"Got it," said TJ, smiling, thinking about how much she already reminded him of his mother.

"Then draw a table and chair set. Look, I have a magazine picture right here," she said, pulling a folded piece of paper from one pocket of her jeans. The round table was made of oak, painted white on the top and with a moss green pedestal base. The chairs were also wooden and painted moss green to match the table. "But we will need five chairs instead of four."

"Give me a few minutes to get these things drawn then we can see what else we need. Okay, kiddo?" said TJ.

"Yeah! I can't wait to see everything," Claudia said.

It did not take TJ long to use the *Furniture* pencil and fill the room. Everything fit the spaces perfectly.

"We have room for a couple more things," said Claudia. "Can you draw a mahogany bookcase to fit on this wall? This way we have a place to put books and magazines and games, without leaving everything on the floor or the table."

"Sure," said TJ.

"And then can you draw a large square trunk that is big enough to put things like our skateboards in? It could fit right here in front of the sofas and also be like a coffee table."

"I think I can do that, but then that's enough furniture. We still want to have space to hang out," TJ said, as he got started on the last two requests.

"Once we add these last two things, the fort will be perfect!" said Claudia.

TJ had just finished the trunk, when Matthew called from the rooftop, "Hey TJ, can you bring those pencils up here and draw some lounge chairs?"

"I'm hungry," David said, coming down the stairs. "We have this great table and chairs. Let's eat some snacks first."

"Better yet, why don't I use the *Food* pencil to draw two delicious pizzas, one cheese and one pepperoni?" suggested TJ. "Then I promise, Matthew, I will come up and draw lounge chairs, and you can hang out on the roof and watch for enemy spies."

"Draw the pizzas. I'm coming down!" said Matthew.

The pizza, like the gingerbread house, was delicious. The kids thought about having TJ draw some dessert, but instead opted for another pizza, with half plain cheese and half pepperoni. By the time they finished eating, no one had room for dessert.

As promised, TJ drew lounge chairs for the roof space. It did not take very long before David and Matthew, with full bellies, were happy on the rooftop. Claudia curled up on the new sofa and dozed off.

TJ and Stephen tried to figure out the location of the secret vault.

"I have looked at every crack and crevice in this place and cannot find the safe," said Stephen. "Are you sure there is one?"

"Positive," said TJ. "I remember drawing it around this interior staircase. I just can't remember how I drew the access to open it. Let's pull on the metal handles and the stone steps, and see if anything happens."

Individually, they tried a few combinations. "Hey, I have an idea," said TJ. "You pull on two of the metal handles on the right side of the steps, and I'll pull on two on the left. Let's see if there is a combination that will open something up."

It took them a few tries, but finally it worked. When both boys had their hands on the handles next to the sixth step and the seventh step, and pulled on them at the same time, the steps and the stone between opened outward.

"Cool," said Stephen. "The space isn't huge, but you could definitely hide the pencils in here and some money."

TJ was impressed with the way the pencils had brought to life everything he'd thought about when he was drawing. "I can't believe the pencils created this secret space, just by my thinking about it," said TJ.

"It is interesting that you have to have two people to open it," said Stephen. "One person could not pull on all four handles at once. I guess this way no one can conceal something from everyone else. At least one other person has to help you hide it away."

"I like it," said TJ. "It forces us to trust each other. I can't wait to show it to the others."

Shortly after the discovery of the vault, Claudia woke up and Stephen and TJ showed everyone how to open it. The kids spent the next hour trying to figure out if there were any other secrets in their new fort.

By the time they'd finished exploring and playing, it was close to dinner time. TJ did not want to get into any more trouble with his parents. "Guys, I think we should start heading back. We don't want Mom to worry."

"Should I bring the skateboards up here for the night, to be sure nothing happens to them?" Stephen asked.

"I think they are fine where they are," said David. "They have been hidden in the tall grass under twigs for two weeks without anyone bothering them. I agree with TJ; we should start heading back. Mom would probably like having us back a little early for dinner."

"Can we each go down the slide one more time?" Claudia asked.

"Definitely!" said David.

They decided to leave the tools and other supplies stored neatly on the shelves of the bookcase. They agreed that they would not leave food in the fort, because they did not want to attract bugs or other creepy creatures. So they packed up the remainder of their snacks, took a ride down the slide, and headed out of the woods toward home.

Chapter 9
Kindness

The children were still a good distance from their house when they noticed their neighbor, Mrs. Watkins, standing in the street next to her car.

"Mrs. Watkins, are you okay?" David asked.

"Oh heavens, you kids are a sight for sore eyes," Mrs. Watkins said. "I was just on my way home from the grocery store and my car got this flat tire. I have no idea what to do. I've called my son several times, but he isn't answering. I'm really worried all this food I just bought is going to spoil."

"Hey, no problem," said David, turning to look at the flat tire on the rear of the driver's side. "We help our dad with stuff like this all the time. Let's open the back and see what kind of spare you have. We can take the flat tire off and put the spare on. You should be all set before any of your food goes bad."

"Oh my goodness, you children are a life saver," she replied, opening the trunk.

TJ quickly pulled David and Matthew aside and said, "Hey, do you think you can keep her over on the passenger side for a few minutes? I'm going to try to use the *Equipment* pencil and make her a new tire."

"Are you sure that's safe?" David asked.

"Well, we will know almost right away. If the tire does not inflate, then I erase it, and we go to plan b and help her with the spare."

"Okay," said David, nodding. "I like it."

Matthew and Claudia kept Mrs. Watkins distracted as they moved her groceries out of the trunk and into the back seat, so that the David could access the jack stored under the trunk floor. He and Stephen used the jack to prop the car up, and then removed the old tire.

Meanwhile, TJ knew he didn't have much time. As soon as David and Stephen had the old tire off, he needed to be ready to draw the new one. While the others worked, he carefully looked at the rim of the front tire. He noted the brand and the model of the tire. He was not sure if it would make a difference, but he wanted to be as exact as possible when drawing the details.

David and Stephen got the tire off quickly, and just as fast, TJ worked with the pencils. Before the groceries were unloaded, a new fully inflated tire had popped off the pad of paper and landed positioned in place of the old tire.

David refastened the lug nuts using the tire iron. Then very carefully, he used the jack to lower the car to the ground. Miraculously, the tire remained inflated.

The boys high-fived each other, proud of their good deed.

"I have to admit, I was doubtful this would work," said David.

"Honestly, I was too," said TJ. "I didn't think it would stay inflated. I was really worried when you were lowering the car back to the ground."

Matthew, Claudia, and Mrs. Watkins had finished with the groceries and were talking about the fireworks show that the city put on every Fourth of July. "I just love the big ones that fill the sky with light," Mrs. Watkins said, as David approached.

"Okay, you're all set," David announced as he led Mrs. Watkins around to the side of her car to see her new tire.

"Well that was certainly fast," she said. "You boys really are something else."

"The good news is that you had an extra full size tire back here, so your spare tire is still tucked away," said David. "We put the flat tire in the back of your car. Your son can check it out, but my guess is that it was worn down. The treads are really low here. You should probably have all the others looked at soon."

"What a stroke of good luck that you children were here," said Mrs. Watkins. "I never pay attention to these things. Mr. Watkins always took care of the cars. Since he passed away, I've just been lucky that nothing has happened. I will get this car over to the service station first thing in the morning."

"We are always right next door if you need anything ma'am," David said.

"Absolutely," TJ added. "Just call our mom; we are always happy to help."

"Especially if it has to do with cars," said Stephen, smiling.

Matthew led Mrs. Watkins to her car and opened the door for her before she got behind the wheel.

"Just drive slow and carefully," said David.

"Thanks kids," Mrs. Watkins said as she waved out the window.

"Did you draw that tire, Thomas Joseph?" Claudia asked.

"Yes, I did. I am trying to use these pencils only for good and not evil," TJ said with a twinkle in his eye.

The children continued and were only a few blocks from home when they saw a kid in Claudia's class walking with his arms full of blankets.

"Hey, isn't that Jacob Wynn from your class, Claudia?" Matthew asked.

"I think so," said Claudia. "What's he is doing with all those blankets? Hey Jacob," she hollered. "What are you doing? Do you need help?"

The boy was barely able to see the kids coming up the street, over all the blankets in his arms. "Hey guys," he said. "I am going around to houses collecting old blankets for the animal shelter downtown. My mom and I volunteer there once a month. We were helping out yesterday and the vets said they wanted old blankets for all the kennels."

"Wow! That is super generous of you. How long ago did you start working there?" Claudia asked.

While Claudia continued her conversation with the boy, TJ started planning a way to help. He pulled his brothers aside. "Guys, what do you think about helping Jacob out? I could draw him a wagon, so he can easily haul the blankets."

"Nice, but then we should also draw him a bunch of blankets, so he can add them to the pile and take them to the shelter," said David.

"Which pencils would you use for all the drawings?" Stephen asked. "Would the wagon be considered equipment or a toy? And what about blankets, which pencil would you use for that?"

"I think the *Equipment* pencil would be the best choice for the wagon. It is a piece of equipment that will carry things," said TJ.

"Okay, but what about the blankets?" Stephen asked again.

"I don't really know," TJ said. "Maybe the *Clothing* pencil, since blankets are made out of cloth and sometimes old clothing, like quilts."

"Sounds good," said David. "It looks like Claudia's got him pretty interested in their conversation. Why don't Stephen, Matthew, and I stand here and block the view, while you draw?"

TJ agreed and immediately got to work. He used the *Equipment* pencil first and within two minutes, was done with his sketch. TJ had tried to keep the wagon from looking brand new. He wanted Jacob to think it was an old wagon they had, that they didn't need any more. He even imagined in his mind that the name *Binder* was written in black lettering on the bottom of the wagon.

When the wagon appeared, TJ carefully looked it over, noticing it had the slightly worn look he was hoping it would have, as well as their family name scribed on the bottom.

With one part of the project done, TJ hurried to finish phase two. He put the *Equipment* pencil away and took out the *Clothing* pencil. There were five Binder kids, so TJ decided to draw five blankets, one from each kid. He got creative and drew each blanket so it had a design or pattern on it that represented that child. In his mind he imagined David's blanket covered with pictures of tools, Stephen's covered with images of money, Matthew's covered with army tanks, Claudia's covered with stuffed animals, and his own blanket with pictures of different colored pencils.

As each blanket was drawn and brought to life, it made a little whoosh and landed stretched over the top of the wagon. David hurried to grab them as they came off the page, then he turned to his brothers and quickly they folded them as best they could and placed them in the wagon. Before long the blankets and the wagon were ready to go.

David called to Claudia and Jacob, "Hey guys, we were just talking and thought we'd give our picnic blankets to you, Jacob."

"Wow guys! That is really awesome. Are you sure you don't need these blankets?" Jacob asked.

"We are certain," said Stephen. "Our grandmother sends us new blankets each year for Christmas. We have extras of these hanging around. I am sure our mom won't mind."

Claudia smiled at her brothers. "You guys are so thoughtful."

"Hey, why don't you take the wagon with you too?" said TJ. "We hardly ever use it anymore. You can put the other blankets you have in here with these."

"Awesome! It is supposed to start storming in a little while, so this will help me get home before the rain starts," said Jacob. "Then tomorrow I can go around and collect even more!"

"Thanks for looking out for the animals at the shelter, Jacob," said Claudia. "Guys, we better get home or we'll be late for dinner and Mom will not be happy."

"Yep, let's get moving," said TJ. "I do not need to be in trouble again."

As Jacob dumped all his blankets in the wagon, the kids waved good-bye and started on their way.

They got home, just in time for dinner, but Mom was not upset. Mrs. Watkins had called to tell her how her children had saved the day. She said that she planned to send over one of her famous chocolate cakes as a thank you for their kindness.

After dinner, TJ took a quick bath and went to bed. He was exhausted from his long day. As he lay in bed, he thought about the good that had come from his using the pencils. The fort was a great get away for his siblings, and the tire had helped out Mrs. Watkins. The blankets and wagon had put a huge smile on Jacob's face, and would soon make a bunch of dogs and cats very happy.

From inside his safe warm house, TJ could hear the rumble of thunder outside. Although he had enjoyed using the pencils today, he really was looking forward to getting back to the ramp and the skateboards, and to painting designs without any magic. Hopefully the storm would be gone by morning and he could spend the day outside playing.

Chapter 10
Plans

At breakfast, Mom had gone upstairs to pull sheets off the bed for washing. This left the kids with the chance to speak freely about their plans for the day.

"Who's ready to get back to work on the ramp?" Stephen asked.

All his siblings nodded yes or raised their hand. "I love the fort and I felt great about helping others, but I want to finish the project we started together, and get the ramp finished," said David.

"Yeah, I really like the pencils, but I am ready to get the ramp finished too, and show you all who the best Binder skateboarder is in this family," said Matthew.

"Agreed, no pencils today," said TJ. "I can't wait to try out some new moves and do just what Matthew said: show who the best skateboarder is in this family."

Ready to go back out to the empty lot, the kids put away their breakfast dishes, put their supplies together, and headed off toward the McAllister's farm.

As they walked, TJ asked each kid what kind of design they wanted painted on their skateboard. As a group, they decided to have TJ paint a dragon on the ramp and the words, *Fire Breathers Rule.*

Everyone was looking forward to the day ahead, but the good mood and excitement were suddenly cut short as they suddenly saw what lay ahead, or rather—what was missing. After passing the wooded area and turning into the clearing, they noticed the ramp was gone!

"Our ramp!" David shouted, as he ran toward the spot where it had stood.

TJ and his siblings all ran behind David. They found the metal support system on the ground in pieces. As they surveyed the area, they saw the billboard that had been serving as the ramp lying flat in the field, about ten yards from where they left it.

"Who do you think did this?" Matthew asked.

"I don't know," replied David. "I'm not even sure it's a who. It could've been a what. The wind from the storm last night could have caught the ramp and sent it flying."

"But look at this," TJ remarked as he held up some of the screws and bolts. "It looks like someone was getting ready to strip this thing of the hardware before the storm came along." The screws showed marks where a screwdriver had stripped the x on top of them. David had taught the kids a long time ago to avoid damaging the top of the screw, so you could remove it later.

TJ was furious, thinking that someone had tried to destroy what they had worked so hard to make.

David remained calm and took the screw, shaking his head. "Well not much we can do but try and put this back together again. I found some new screws and hardware in the garage so hopefully, it won't take me that long to fix."

But TJ could not let go of the anger he felt. The idea of someone ruining their hard work made him want to retaliate. It was this tendency, to get irritated so quickly and behave rashly, that often caused him to get into trouble. And today, he was more than just irritated. He and his siblings had been working on this project for over two weeks and now someone had the nerve to come along and ruin it in one afternoon. "That's it!" declared TJ. "This is war. If someone wants to mess with us they better be ready to fight!"

"Thomas Joseph, what are you planning on doing?" Claudia asked cautiously.

"I'm gonna draw a dragon like we talked about. He can stand guard here and make sure nothing happens to our stuff."

"Yeah, a huge real-looking fire-breathing monster that would keep other people away," Matthew agreed.

"Oooh, let's do it, Thomas Joseph!" Claudia said. "I would love a pet dragon."

TJ knew that the others were thinking about a fake dragon, but what TJ was thinking about would be as real as the dog he drew for Claudia. He got out his pencils and paper and started to draw, forgetting all about rule number two on the note with the pencils: *Only use the pencils when you are in a good mood. This is VERY important. The pencils respond to your thoughts and feelings.* In the past TJ had been in a great mood when he used the pencils. For that reason, the fish were timid, the gingerbread fort and pizza tasted delicious, and the dog for Claudia was sweet and friendly. Unfortunately, right now TJ was in a very bad mood.

The kids knew it would take TJ a while to draw something as complicated as a dragon so, while he was sketching, they joined David in collecting what was left of the ramp. Once they had everything together, David emptied the hardware bag with all the extra nuts, bolts, nails, and screws.

"Hey look at TJ," said Matthew.

They walked over to TJ, who was about three-fourths of the way through the drawing. The pencil was positioned so that the label, *Animals*, was visible. "Hey TJ, are you sure you want to draw a real dragon? I thought you were just going to make a fake one to scare people off." But Stephen's observation came too late.

TJ was already deep in his trance-like state and too close to finishing to stop. Claudia, Stephen, Matthew, and David could only watch over his shoulder as he put the final touches on the picture, and wait to see what happened.

The seconds seemed like an eternity until TJ was done. In slow motion, the picture moved from the paper into a three dimensional object, making a poof! But unlike the tiny poof that came from the other drawings, this was an enormous **poof** that made everyone jump backwards. TJ hadn't yet realized that he'd landed his siblings with a major catastrophe.

Chapter 11
Disaster

Immediately, the dragon let out a roar of fury accompanied by a blast of fire. Stunned and frozen in place, the children were covered with soot from the dragon's breath. Just as the rules promised, TJ's bad mood had been conveyed to his art object. Within seconds, the dragon turned his attention away from the children and roared in the direction of the skateboard ramp. Instantly, the billboard sign went up in flames.

"Whadda we do now!?" shrieked Claudia.

"Hey TJ, remember the *Water* pencil!" David yelled, trying to be heard over the dragon's roars.

TJ scrambled around, looking in the box. Miraculously the paper and pencils had not got caught in the dragon's blast. Hurriedly, TJ began to draw big puddles around the ramp site. The puddles were large enough to stop the fire spreading, but they still needed a way to put out the fire on the ramp. Quickly, he plucked the *Equipment* pencil out of the box and drew five large buckets. Then he went back to his *Water* pencil and filled the containers up.

In the background, a large black pick-up truck slowly passed on the street. The driver rolled down his window and brought his car to a stop.

"Great, we have company," Stephen reported, nudging David and Matthew to turn their attention to the street. By the time the boys had turned, the driver had taken out his cell phone, and looked as if he was making a call.

"He is probably calling the fire department," David groaned.

"You think he can see the dragon?" Matthew asked. There was no time for anyone to answer. The buckets had become real and now contained water. Giving no more thought to the truck, each child picked up a bucket and doused the billboard sign, extinguishing the flames.

While the kids were busy, the dragon moved toward the forest. Panting from the heat, the kids surveyed the charred wreckage of their ramp. "Where'd the dragon go?" asked TJ anxiously. Guilt was nibbling at his stomach and he tried to ignore it.

"I don't know, but he's mean!" Claudia said. "What if he burns the forest?"

TJ gulped and squinted into the trees.

The large beast was barely in view.

"We can't lose sight of him. He might hurt someone!" said Claudia.

"Hey, can't you erase him like you did with the gingerbread house?" Matthew asked.

TJ's eyes lit up as he remembered the rubber finger. "Of course I can! Matthew, you are a genius!" But, as suddenly, he also remembered that he had to see the item he was erasing for it to work. "Oh, no!" he yelled. "If we lose him, I can't erase him." He pulled open the box lid and frantically searched for the rubber finger eraser, but it wasn't there. "What? Where did it go?"

"Where did what go?" David asked, panicked.

"The eraser, I must have dropped it! Quick, search the ground for it! It's the only way to destroy the dragon!"

Fire engine sirens sounded in the distance, as the children desperately searched the ground for the eraser.

For a moment, Matthew turned his attention back to the street. "Guys, the truck is gone. He must've phoned for help."

"We can't leave here until I find that eraser!" said TJ. "Look, are those trees on fire? Ugggghhhh!" The dragon was no longer visible, but the path he had taken had been marked by the fire he left behind. Several trees leading into the wooded area were now in flames.

"Okay, you guys quit worrying about the trees and the fire trucks, and just find that eraser. I will deal with the firefighters when they get here, okay?" said David. "You all just go along with whatever story I come up with, *capisce*?"

"*Capisce!*" they all replied.

Stephen spotted the eraser, as three fire trucks pulled up to the scene. He quickly tossed it to TJ who slipped it into his pocket. Within seconds it seemed like the area was swarming with firemen. Luckily, no one stopped to talk to the kids or ask them about the fire. The firefighters headed for the burning trees. TJ heard one of them saying, "MOVE! If those flames get out of control we could have a full-blown forest fire on our hands!" TJ's mind filled with dread. His stomach knotted. He knew he'd acted rashly, not thinking about the consequences of revenge. If Mom and Dad find out, I'll be grounded for days, he thought. I'll miss out on playing in the fort.

For the next thirty minutes or so, the five children stood in silence out of the way of the firemen, watching them. Hoses, and men in yellow jackets, were everywhere. Four more fire trucks arrived.

The children were unsure of what to do. "Where is the picture of the dragon TJ? David asked.

"I shoved it back in my backpack," said TJ. "If I lose the picture we will really be in trouble."

"At least the dragon headed off to the woods on the right and not toward our fort," said Stephen.

"Actually if he headed toward the fort we could use the lookout tower to see him and get him erased," said Matthew. "Unfortunately, you can't see beyond the field."

"Let's wait to make sure the fire is under control. I might have a plan," said TJ.

Slowly, the blaze in the distance disappeared and the firemen retreated to their trucks to put away their equipment. The children started to move from the spot where they had stood watching. TJ reached down for the black box and slipped the eraser inside.

"Hey, let's get out of here before they start asking us a bunch of questions," David said. "TJ, you can tell us your plan on the way home."

But as they turned around, they were called to a halt by a large fireman with his hand out, like a crossing guard stopping traffic.

"Whoa, where you kids going? Why don't you stick around and tell us what happened here?"

As promised, David became the group spokesman. He looked right at the fireman, whose name tag read *Bowers*. "We don't' really know. We just happened to be passing by and saw this piece of wood burning. We were gonna call for help but we didn't have a cell phone. I think some guy driving by in a truck called nine-one-one."

Bowers seemed to only half-listen to David's response. Instead he turned his attention to TJ who just happened to be putting the box into his backpack. "Why don't ya hand me what ya got there boy?" Bowers asked.

But TJ was not about to turn over the magic pencils. Instead he held the box behind his back, locking his gaze with that of the firefighter. Suddenly, he felt the box being ripped from his grasp. Turning, he saw another tall scrawny firefighter, named Pinkers, holding his container of pencils.

"Hey, that's mine," TJ said, reaching out to grab the box back. But he was not quite fast enough to get it from the lanky man.

Pinkers tried to open the box, but could not get the lid to budge. After trying several times to discover the contents of the box, he turned his attention back to TJ. "What's in here?" he asked, raising one eyebrow suspiciously.

"It's mine! It's magic," TJ said without thinking.

"Oh really, magic? Magic what? Magic cards, or no wait, maybe you have some magic beans in here and you're planning on planting them, hoping to grow a great big beanstalk," Pinkers said, his voice dripping with sarcasm.

"Hey that's enough," David said. "He just means he got it as part of a magic kit. It's one of those dumb boxes that won't come apart. They put a couple of rocks in there, so it makes some noise and drives you crazy, but the box is glued closed. Just give it back to him."

"I don't know if I believe you kids. What if you have matches in there and that is how this whole thing got started?" Bowers interjected.

Fortunately, another firefighter, named Steckler, appeared, causing the other men to ease up on the kids. He quietly took the black box from Pinkers' grasp. After looking it over for a minute and trying to open it without any luck, he calmly addressed the children. In a slow southern drawl, he began a much milder line of questioning, beginning with, "Hey kids, thanks for helping us by staying out of the way. What are your names?" Dutifully they all replied, but only Claudia gave her full name including Binder. "Well why don't you all tell me what you saw, so we can help find out who caused this big mess? Maybe you can help us identify who's been out here building a skateboard ramp?"

David replied, "Honest, officer, we just happened to be passing by looking for a place to play kickball without having to worry about my little sister here getting run over by a car. We found this spot and the next thing we knew that piece of wood was on fire."

"And you just happened to have some buckets of water handy?" Steckler asked, pointing toward the wet metal containers.

"No, well, we actually brought them along to help us cool off while we were playing," David said, keeping his tone serious. "I heard on the news the other day that heat stroke can be dangerous, even for little kids.

So, we each decided to bring a bucket filled with water to pour over us when we got too hot. My little sister also brought drinks to keep us hydrated."

"Humph, you kids always come this prepared for a hot day?" Steckler asked.

"Oh, we are very good at playing outside. Our mom encourages it in the summer," David remarked.

"I bet she does. So you just came out here to play kickball and ride skateboards on a ramp when you saw the fire. Is that correct?" Steckler said.

"Oh, no sir, we were just going to play kickball! We don't know anything about that skateboard ramp," David said, not falling for the firefighter's trick.

About that time another firefighter came over and said, "Scott, you might want to have a look at these." In his arms were the five skateboards the kids had made from the wood scraps and roller skating wheels. On the bottom of each was a name: David, TJ, Stephen, Matthew, and Claudia. "I found them covered with a bunch of twigs and grass over in the field."

The kids sighed with dread. In the midst of the chaos they had completely forgotten about their hidden skateboards.

"Well now, that is quite a coincidence," Steckler said slowly, eyeing the children. "Didn't you kids say your names were David, TJ, Stephen, Matthew, and Claudia? Didn't you say your last name was Binder, little girl?"

Claudia had slipped up when she gave him her last name, but she was not falling for any new tricks. She looked right back at the firefighter with her big blue eyes and said nothing. David was doing a great job handling the men and she was happy to let him continue doing so.

David was the first to recover from the discovery of the skateboards. "Wow, hey guys, look, the nice firefighter found our skateboards!" he cheered. "They were stolen from our garage a few weeks ago and we thought for sure we would never see them again. What a lucky day, first we happen to have water buckets and get to help put out a fire, and now we find our stolen skateboards." David stared at his siblings who played along, smiling and exclaiming about their lost skateboards.

Steckler was not fooled though. Since a fire had occurred in the area, he declared it unsafe and a crime scene, telling the kids they could no longer play there until a full investigation and inspection of the trees could be done.

"How about we give you a ride home in a fire truck to make sure you get where you need to go safely?" Steckler suggested. The other firefighters started ushering the kids onto a truck.

The younger children were actually excited to be riding in a real fire truck, but TJ was still worried about getting his pencils back. "Hey can I have my magic box back?"

"Yeah, I tell you what, I'll give it back to you once we get you home safely," Steckler said, shaking the box and making the pencils rattle inside.

"The stolen skateboards too?" David asked.

"Sure, the stolen skateboards too," Steckler promised.

Chapter 12
Trouble

Even though they were covered in soot, and were probably going to be in trouble again, the Binder children enjoyed their escort home in the fire truck. Claudia kept asking to turn on the siren, Stephen wanted to help steer, and Matthew asked to ride on the outside where other kids might see him. Even TJ and David started to relax. It wasn't until the truck pulled up in front of their house, that TJ's enthusiasm was replaced with cold dread.

When Mom answered the door, her face froze in shock. She quickly counted her children. When she realized they were all present and appeared unharmed, her expression changed to irritation. Turning her attention to the firemen, she smiled and in the friendliest voice she could muster, said, "Good afternoon, gentlemen. What can I do for you?"

Fireman Steckler, standing in the center of the group, spoke first. "Good afternoon ma'am. Are these your children?"

"Yes, sir," she replied, still smiling and sounding cheery. "All five of them belong to me."

"Well ma'am," the firefighter said, "Your children seemed to have been involved in some sort of mishap today, over by the McAllister's farm, on the other side of the creek. They were a little to the north of the farm, where it's kinda isolated. You know, it's where they started building that new subdivision, the one that got put on hold when the contractor skipped town with all the money. You probably heard about it in the news."

Mom nodded and said pleasantly, "Yes, I know the area you are referring to."

"Well ma'am, sometime around noon today a ramp, a skateboard ramp that is, caught on fire and spread flames into some of the nearby trees. Fortunately, a local guy happened to be passing by and called nine-one-one. We were able to control the flames and put out the fire without too much damage."

TJ crossed all his fingers behind his back, wishing for some miracle to prevent Mom from spotting the skateboards. No such luck. Mom glanced at the firefighter to the left, holding the boards. She took a deep breath that she let out slowly, indicating that she was prepared to hear whatever other news this man was about to share. "Go on, please."

"Well ma'am, your children happened to be found at the scene," said Steckler. "They claim that these skateboards had been stolen from the garage of your house and coincidently left by the ramp that caught on fire, but that they knew nothing about the ramp before today. They also claim they just happened to each have a bucket full of water that they used to extinguish the flames on the ramp. They said they routinely bring buckets of water outside with them, so they don't get heat stroke. We asked them several times what happened, but it seems besides giving me their names and asking to drive the fire truck, no one was willing to talk expect the oldest one here."

Mom continued to listen, her eyes scanning her children. The boys looked at the ground and Claudia stared up at the sky.

Steckler said, "We cannot press any charges against them, mostly because we have no evidence that contradicts their statements, but also because they are minors. However, we want to make them aware of the fact that they could have been seriously injured today. We want them know that arson, setting fire to something, is a felony and is punishable by time in jail and would go on their permanent record if they were found guilty. In addition, it is against the local ordinance to build or construct a skateboard ramp."

"I really apologize for any involvement my children might have had in this incident today," said Mom. Maybe they were simply in the wrong place at the wrong time. Their father and I have repeatedly told them they are not to go over to the area you mentioned for the very reason that something could happen and they would have no way of getting help." Mom stopped and looked at her children before continuing, "Their father and I will certainly talk to them tonight. Thank you so much for getting them home safely."

That seemed to satisfy the firemen, but before they left the one to the right held out a black box. "Here ma'am," he said. "We believe this, and those skateboards over there," he indicated by nodding in the direction of the firefighter on the left, "belong to your children."

"Thank you," Mom said, taking the box, but watching her children. To them she said, "Inside, now," in a voice that let them know she was not buying the story they'd told the firefighters, and that they were indeed in trouble.

Chapter 13
Confession

Upstairs the kids had taken baths and put on clean clothes. TJ made sure the one picture of the dragon was still in his backpack. He took all the other pictures he had drawn with the magic pencils and stacked them neatly in his the top drawer of his desk. He would be sure to put all the images in the treehouse vault, the next time they were there.

While waiting for their parents to call them downstairs, the kids assembled in David and TJ's room. They were trying to think of ways to find the dragon without anyone having to get too close.

"What if you draw a ladder that goes to the top of a really tall tree and we can watch from there," said Claudia.

"The ladder could tip over," said David.

TJ had been thinking about a plan since the fire started. "I've got an idea, guys, but it may be hard to convince Mom and Dad it is a good one."

Before he got a chance to share it, Dad called up, "Kids, come on down here. Your mother and I would like to speak with you."

"Don't worry, guys, this time I'll do the talking," TJ said, as they headed to the den.

Their parents stared at them in silence until they wriggled with discomfort. "What's going on?" Dad finally asked.

TJ looked squarely back at his parents. "We are willing to tell you everything that happened, and even prove we are telling the truth, you must promise to will help us. Okay?"

"TJ, your mother and I may not always like what you kids do, but we do love you, and will always be willing to help when you're in trouble," Dad replied.

"You may change your mind," TJ warned, "because right now, we are in BIG trouble."

"TJ, you're scaring me! Just tell us what happened," said Mom.

"Okay," he said looking at the other kids before sharing their story. He began with finding the pencils in the trash, learning they were magic, taking them to the abandoned neighborhood, the attack on the skateboard ramp, (which they apologized for building), then followed up with the creation of the dragon and ended with the ride on the fire truck. He left out the part about the sugar fort, the fish tank, the tree fort, and even their day of good deeds. These were details that were not essential to the story right now.

By the time TJ was done with his explanation, Dad and Mom looked like they were torn between disbelief and serious concern.

"Let me get this straight," Dad clarified. "You found some magic pencils that you used to draw a fire-breathing dragon to protect your illegal skateboard ramp. But the dragon burned down the ramp and some trees, and is now on the loose in the woods. Is that about right?"

"Yes," the children mumbled, nodding.

"And now you need us to help you catch this dragon before he hurts anyone else."

"Yes," the children replied again.

Dad sighed, rubbing his forehead. "I don't know about you, Carol, but I need a little more proof." He looked over at his wife, who nodded in agreement. "Where are the pencils and the picture of the dragon now?"

"Mom has the pencils. The picture of the drawing is in my backpack with my extra paper," TJ said.

"I'll go get the pencils, TJ you go get your backpack. You are going to need paper, and I want to see what this dragon looks like," said Mom.

Within a few minutes, Mom was handing TJ the box of pencils. Before she did though, she tried to open the lid to see if it was true that only TJ had been able to take the top off. The lid would not budge. Moments later she watched as TJ took off the lid with ease.

TJ showed his parents the picture of the dragon. "I'm going to hold on to this," said Dad.

TJ handed over the picture of the dragon and took out his extra paper. "Okay, what do you want me to draw?" TJ asked.

"Well, what are my choices?" Mom asked.

"Pretty much anything," and then TJ rattled off the titles etched in the sides of the pencils. "*Animals, Land, Equipment, Plants, Food, Water, Transportation, Clothing, Beverages, Structures, Toys,* or *Furniture,* take your pick."

"*Furniture*?" she asked raising her eyebrows in satisfaction. "What if you make me a new coffee table since you kids have basically destroyed this one with your dirty shoes?"

"Sure," TJ said looking at his dad who nodded in agreement.

TJ selected the *Furniture* pencil from the box and flipped his drawing pad to a clean sheet of paper. The others cleared the floor in the den to make room for the new table. TJ began sketching. As he drew, the tip of the pencil swirled with different shades of black and brown.

TJ's facial expression became fixed as he concentrated intently. Just as it had in the past, his hand flew across the page in a fluid motion that made it seem what he was doing was so simple. The lines on the page began to take shape and within a few minutes a beautiful, solid, square mahogany coffee table, with side drawers and nickel-plated knobs, adorned the page.

"That's really beautiful," Mom said, looking over his shoulder, sounding impressed.

The children, who had already witnessed the work of the magic pencils, knew to look toward the clear space for the coffee table to appear. David signaled to his parents to move their attention to the area in the center of the room. The timing was perfect. Just as Mom and Dad lifted their gaze away from the page and toward the empty space, the hand-drawn image bubbled up into a three dimensional figure before completely popping off the page and landing on the floor of the den.

The coffee table was every bit as gorgeous in real life as it had been in the picture. "Oh my, oh my, oh TJ! It's stunning!" Mom said, as she moved toward the new furniture. She stroked the top to feel the smooth finish of the wood, and gently pulled open the drawers, getting wafts of the soft scent of newness coming from inside. "Can you do more like this?"

Dad stood looking stunned. "I can't believe it," he said in awe. Neither one was quite sure what to do next.

TJ gave them a moment to digest what just happened before bringing them back to reality. "Yeah, well if you think this is impressive, just wait til you see the angry dragon I made."

Shocked back to the problem at hand, Mom moaned, "Oh geez TJ, you *really* drew an angry dragon? What were you thinking?"

TJ was about to speak, but David stepped in to help. "Mom, come on, you and Dad promised you wouldn't be mad. Look, we know it was not very smart, and we are really sorry, but we need your help. TJ has an idea." David looked back at TJ who knew it was time to propose his solution.

"Well we know *how* to get rid of it, what we need to do is *locate* it so we can erase it," said TJ.

"What do you mean 'erase' it?" Dad asked.

TJ explained about the eraser. "Here, I'll erase the coffee table and show you how it works."

"No you will not!" Mom interjected, wedging her body between TJ and the coffee table as if to defend it. "I like this coffee table, and it is staying right where it is. What else did you kids draw? I'm sure there are other things we can erase. Why don't we search and find some of your treasures to get rid of, huh? In fact, I bet you can explain how a fish tank suddenly appeared in your bedroom."

David and TJ shifted uncomfortably in their seats.

"That's right, I got a call from Missy Adams earlier today saying they were staying in town and did not need us to get the fish tank. So, if the Adam's fish tank is not upstairs, I bet I can guess how one suddenly *did* get upstairs."

Dad spoke up. "Honey, do we really need to see the eraser work at this point?" He shook his head no to answer his own question. "Kids, we believe you. Let's just figure out our next steps." He paused before adding, "Man, I really thought you were making this whole thing up."

"Dad, the next step is where you and Mom come in. I have an idea, but we are going to need your help. Mom, didn't you tell

Claudia that you used to fly helicopters for the army?"

Chapter 14
Mission

Last year Claudia had made a discovery that stunned her brothers. While asking Mom questions about how she met their father, Claudia learned that her mother had served in the United States Army, and had worked as a helicopter pilot. She also learned their dad used to dangle from helicopters on a rappel rope to rescue soldiers.

At the time, TJ found the information about his mother most surprising. He had always assumed she never had a real job. Today, however, he figured that his mother's previous experience was perfect for helping him find the dragon.

"Mom, I need you to help fly a chopper over the woods so I can erase the dragon. Dad, I need your help getting me securely strapped to the side," TJ said.

"TJ, we don't have a helicopter," Mom said.

"I remember Claudia saying that you showed her old blueprints of the helicopter you used to fly. If you show those to me, I can draw it, then poof, you can fly it."

"TJ, I appreciate your idea, and I think it is a very creative one, but hanging out of a metal bird is not that easy," said Mom.

"We would also need other safety equipment to make all this happen," added Dad.

"So I will use the *Transportation* pencil to draw the helicopter, and the *Equipment* pencil for all the other stuff," said TJ, confidently.

"Awesome! We can call this the Binder Family Mission," said Stephen.

"TJ, I don't think you understand how dangerous this could be," said Mom. "It is one thing to have a coffee table made by magic pencils. If it suddenly disappears, then the worst situation I might be facing is a stained carpet. A magic helicopter is an entirely different risk, one that I am not willing to take with my family."

TJ said, "Mom, I made that aquarium two days ago and it is still here. If the magic does wear off, it doesn't happen suddenly and we should only be in the air for about thirty minutes."

"What if you accidently draw one part wrong so we suddenly come crashing down?" Mom asked.

"If I accidently draw something wrong, it won't take off in the first place," said TJ. "Mom, I understand your worry, but let's give it a try. I can draw all the things we need, and if you really don't think it will work, we can try another plan. Right now, this is the best shot we have."

TJ watched as his parents looked at one another. He saw his mom raise one eyebrow at his dad, which meant she was thinking about it. He then saw his dad wink, which meant he thought the plan might work.

"Yes!" said TJ. "I promise, I will be extra careful with the drawings."

For the next few minutes, TJ sat with his parents and they came up with a plan.

Everyone had a role except Claudia. Mom, Dad, and TJ agreed that she would have to stay strapped into a chair inside the cabin of the chopper. David would be given a quick tutorial and asked to help co-pilot. TJ, Matthew, and Stephen would join Dad and be attached to rappel gear, and help scope for the fire-breathing monster.

Beforehand, they were going to need TJ to use the magic pencils, specifically the *Land, Equipment,* and *Transportation* pencils, to create everything needed to fulfill their mission. Dad and Mom had spent years encouraging their children to trust one another. But today, the adults needed to be willing to take a leap of faith. For the mission to be successful, they'd have to place the same level of confidence in their kids as they had taught their kids to have in each other.

Quickly, Mom and Dad went around the house collecting items, mostly drawings and pictures. TJ was told to find the largest pad of paper he had and bring it as well. Everyone loaded into the family mini-van and headed to the abandoned lot on the other side of the McAllister's farm. As Mom drove, not a word was spoken, but everyone's heart raced, and lots of hands and feet tapped and twitched.

In the field, Dad called David, Stephen, Matthew, and Claudia over to brief them on the operation. Mom took TJ to the side, along with the pictures and his black box of magic pencils. Together, they sat on the ground as Mom showed TJ the equipment they would need, item by item. Most of the equipment was fairly easy for TJ to draw. After his mother described each item, he would take a few minutes and close his eyes. In his mind the item would come to life. The details and descriptions his mother gave him allowed him to see the object in a three dimensional way. Then, seconds after opening his eyes, he would begin to draw with his hand. Each time, the pencil would take over. He felt the pencil guide his movements as the picture slowly appeared on the page. When he was done, his hand would come to an abrupt stop, and within seconds the image would come to life. When the item appeared, it was inspected by Mom first, and then handed to Dad for a second inspection. After it passed the two inspections, Dad took it and explained its purpose and use to the other children.

TJ tried to remain focused, but in between drawings, he imagined what his parents must have been like as a team in the army. Mom and Dad were detailed and calm as they inspected the equipment and gave instructions. They reminded the children that during an operation each person had a specific role that they needed to follow and that there was no room for error. TJ felt respect for how they must have worked and trained their old team in the military. He also felt proud that they were entrusting him and his siblings with the same level of responsibility.

Once Mom and TJ had created all the equipment, they turned their focus to the landscape.

"Will the picture pop to life and just land on top of the rough and rocky lot right here?" Mom wondered out loud.

"I'm not sure. I think it will replace the tiny trees, hills, and holes that are out here. If you describe the exact kind of landing pad you need, I will try to visualize it and draw it," TJ suggested.

"Ideally, this whole area in front of us needs to be level and smooth with just plain grass on top. Anything uneven could cause me to bounce when we are landing," she said.

"Roger," TJ said, excited to see how this pencil could be used. He found it hard to imagine how an entire area of space could be cleared just by drawing it with a pencil. He was not sure how to set the boundaries for this drawing. He decided to include the surrounding land features. Ultimately, TJ wanted to clear the whole area in one picture, and avoid drawing dozens of small pictures of grass trying to patch together.

TJ took a few minutes with his eyes closed to make sure the visual image in his mind was strong enough to guide the pencil. As soon as he had a grasp on the *Land* pencil, his fingers began to tingle. The tip of this pencil was a swirl of green, with slight hues of gold and brown.

Mom watched over TJ's shoulder. As he worked, his fingers moved fluidly over the surface of the paper. The tip of the pencil left streaks of green on the page that looked more like spinach in a blender than a field of grass. Then other colors started entering the picture. On the left side of the page, the barrier of trees that marked the beginning of the woods became visible. On the top of the page he drew more trees to set the northern edge of the field. Unlike pictures in the past, this image was covering the entire sheet of paper. Little by little, every tiny space of white was filled in with shades of green and images of landscape. Toward the end of the drawing, TJ's hand was moving almost too fast to see. From side to side, and up and down the page, it flew until suddenly it stopped.

When TJ's hand came to a rest, the setting illustrated on the page was breathtaking. The grass was perfect! Almost immediately, his thoughts were interrupted as his whole body started shaking. Suddenly nervous about what he might have done, he looked at his mom for reassurance. Before he could say anything, a loud rippling sound started.

The entire family looked in the direction of the noise to witness the land rolling like waves in the ocean. As the grass and trees appeared to flow toward them, the physical features of the land changed before their very eyes. There was nothing subtle about this transformation. The trees to the north and west started rocking, the ground in front of them began cracking, and if they all didn't know any better, they would have thought they were standing over a fault line and experiencing an earthquake.

The earth moved quicker and quicker. The whole process only took a few seconds. At the end, the waves ebbed and came to a standstill. Once everything had settled down, the Binder family looked around and saw a beautiful open field of grass. It appeared as if it had been professionally groomed. If there were no other tasks at hand, they probably would have stood staring for longer, but they were quickly reminded that the field was part of a plan to catch a very angry dragon as a loud *rooaarrr* came from somewhere in the woods.

"Well, at least we know he is still close by," Dad said. "Carol, get TJ started on that bird. I am just about done prepping these guys."

"Got it," Mom agreed.

"TJ, this is the most important drawing you will ever do," Mom said, as she rolled out a large detailed blueprint of a military helicopter. TJ looked directly at his mother and they locked eyes. The idea that his mother, the same woman who was playing bridge with old ladies yesterday, could fly a helicopter seemed unbelievable.

Then it all made sense. His mother was a real person. She knew more than just how to make him clean his room and take a bath. In fact, now that he thought about it, his mother flying a helicopter seemed perfectly reasonable. She never seemed nervous. She definitely got angry and occasionally worried, but his mother was never a nail-biting, fretting, nervous mom. When the boys did get hurt or something was seriously wrong, she was always very calm. And sure, the Crazy Lady came out when she was really aggravated or annoyed, but in a real crisis, like today, she had nerves of steel. He had always had a lot of respect for his mom, but watching her work today, took that feeling to a whole new level. He was determined to make her proud.

"Okay, I guess I am switching to the *Transportation* pencil?" TJ asked.

"Let's do it. I know you will get it right TJ," said Mom, boosting his confidence. Then before he started to draw, she took his face in both of her hands and kissed it three times. "I love you, I love you, I love you," she said after each kiss. "Don't you ever forget it," she whispered into his ear.

Mom spent a long time going over the details of the helicopter. It took her longer to describe it TJ than for him to sketch it. As the *Transportation* pencil flew across the page, silver strokes glowed, slowly producing a magnificent machine.

Close by, Dad and the other kids were almost finished reviewing the basics of flying in a helicopter. Dad reviewed the same skills which he had taught to numerous military and SWAT officers. Matthew, Stephen, and David asked questions as they listened. At the end of the lesson, Dad made each boy repeat the information back to him.

TJ finished the picture as Dad and the kids joined him. After the noisy transformation of the land, they waited to see what kind of an entrance the helicopter would make. It was not long before the image was bubbling up on the page.

Suddenly, VOOOSH!

Before anyone could say, "abracadabra," a perfectly spotless military helicopter was positioned in the middle of the green pasture.

Chapter 15
Search

As soon as the huge silver bird popped off the page, Mom headed over to it, leaving TJ behind with Dad, and calling David to join her. Before David walked away, he asked TJ, "Are you sure this is going to work?"

TJ was surprised by the question. David was always the confident one, the one who kept everyone else from being worried. TJ knew his response had to be convincing. "Absolutely, and you are going to be a natural in the cockpit. I predict you are going to do such a great job and love it so much, you'll be begging to fly again soon," TJ reassured him.

"Thanks, man," David said, patting TJ on the shoulder before walking toward their mother.

When David left, Dad had Stephen and Matthew explain to TJ how the rappel gear worked and what they were going to do once they were in the air. Stephen and Matthew explained the plan for the mission, how to use the safety equipment, and how to manipulate the rope. They showed TJ how to make a Swiss seat out of a rappel rope.

Dad and the three boys, along with Claudia, made their way to the helicopter. Right before getting onboard, Dad yelled at TJ, "Hand me the eraser."

TJ tried to explain to his father that the rules indicated that only TJ should use the items in the box. With the roar overhead, Dad could not fully understand what he was saying.

"TJ, we don't have time for this. It is too dangerous for you to try and hang on the side of the chopper and erase a picture. I will do it," he yelled.

"But Dad, the rules say …" TJ started to yell back.

"I don't want to hear any more excuses, hand me the eraser," Dad ordered.

Reluctantly, TJ handed the eraser over to his father.

Once the issue with the eraser was settled, Mom emerged from the cockpit to get everyone onboard. With David in the co-pilot chair, TJ, Stephen, Matthew, and Claudia got into position, ready for take-off.

From the cockpit Mom hollered back to the cabin, "Tom, check to make sure Claudia is strapped in tightly, and then give me the signal so we can get rolling. We are working on a limited amount of fuel and need to get in the air quickly if you want me to bring us all back safely."

Dad carefully checked Claudia's buckle, then made sure all rappel ropes were hooked with a metal clasp to the chopper, and the boys were securely fastened to the ropes. They each had a parachute pack attached to their back and a pair of binoculars dangling around their neck. They sat on the sides of the helicopter and held on to a handle. Stephen and Matthew were on one side of the chopper, and Dad and TJ were on the other. Once they were ready, Dad signaled in the mirror to Mom that they were clear for takeoff.

TJ had never been so nervous and so excited at the same time. I hope this isn't another rash goof-up that's going to make trouble for everyone, he thought.

"This is just like we've imagined before!" David yelled.

TJ nodded. This quest was similar to the scenarios that they came up with when they played army, but never in a million years had they thought they would be on a real life mission in a helicopter. This would go down as one of the best summers of their young lives. *IF* everything goes as planned, TJ thought. He gulped nervously and scanned the forest for the dragon. *My* dragon, he thought. The one I should never have made.

As they lifted off, TJ looked over at his dad. He had the picture of the dragon taped to the front of his shirt. The tip of the eraser poked out of his pants pocket. Although TJ gave Dad credit for thinking of a clever way to erase the dragon, he was still unsure what would happen when his dad tried to use the eraser. Would it work?

Following the smooth lift off, Mom maneuvered the chopper up and over the trees so the boys would have a visual advantage in trying to find the dragon. TJ looked over the sides of the chopper, relieved the wooded area was not so large. He hoped it would not take them long to spot the beast. The helicopter was flying steady and had just started hovering around the trees when TJ saw the dragon. "Got him!" he yelled.

Inside the helicopter cabin, TJ signaled to the others where to look. Soon, Dad, Stephen, and Matthew had all shown a thumbs-up to indicate that they knew where the dragon was hiding. The next step of the plan was for Mom to keep the aircraft as steady as possible while Dad used the eraser. In the meantime, TJ, Stephen, and Matthew were supposed to keep their binoculars focused on the target in case he moved or tried to run out of sight. Fortunately, the dragon appeared to have settled down for a nap, despite the noise from above.

Although TJ was supposed to watch the dragon, he could not help but stare at his father as he got ready to use the eraser. TJ had a horrible feeling in the pit of his stomach that somehow this was all going to go wrong. If only he had convinced his father that he should be the one to erase the dragon, he would have felt much better.

With the helicopter steadied out, Dad reached into his pocket and withdrew the eraser. TJ watched as his father attempted to erase the dragon. With one hand he gripped the side of the chopper, while the other hand firmly held the rubber, finger-shaped eraser. The rappel ropes, attached to Dad and each of the boys, dangled beneath the helicopter.

At first, it seemed as though the mission was going to be successful. Dad pushed the rubber finger over TJ's sketch and the eraser started to generate tiny sparks. But in a split second everything changed. The instructions had given a direct warning: *These items should never be used by someone who is unable to remove the lid of the box.* Now the warning had been ignored, and trouble began. The sparks that started out as gentle bursts of friction became flames that engulfed Dad's hand.

Dad's reflexes kicked in and he immediately jerked his hand away from the picture. Fortunately, the drawing had been secured to his body and was not at risk of falling, but the eraser was a different story. When his hand caught fire, his palm and fingers popped open, projecting the eraser up into the air. It was as if the events were part of a movie being shown in slow motion. The eraser arced upward from Dad's hand, stalled momentarily in the sky, and then plunged toward the ground. Suddenly, time stopped and everything was frozen in place.

Chapter 16
Plunge

The moment time stood still was one TJ would never forget. The blades of the helicopter stopped spinning, the wind quit blowing, and his family was frozen in place, motionless. It was as if TJ was taken out of his body and floated in air, watching yet another page in the story of his life. As he stood immobile among his family, he noticed that the pattern was always the same. First, an event would trigger powerful emotions, like anger or frustration, in him. Next, he would respond impulsively, creating a mess. Finally, someone else would step in to clean things up. Usually his siblings, but sometimes his parents, helped to bail him out of whatever trouble he'd created.

Over the years he had been warned so many times that the voices of his family echoed in his head, with Claudia saying, "Thomas Joseph, this is a bad idea!"

His mom warning, "Don't even think about it!"

His dad cautioning, "Son, that is only going to get you in trouble!"

David threatening, "TJ, don't you dare..."

Stephen stating, "This is gonna cost you, man!"

Or Matthew assuring him, "There will be serious payback for this!"

He was always in trouble with someone. Only this time he had really done it. The scene before him said it all. His whole family was risking their lives, flying in a helicopter made by magic pencils, and his father was dangling above the trees with his hand on fire. Why do I always do this? he wondered, finally taking responsibility for the events in his life. He should have never allowed his dad to try and erase the picture. It was a mess that he made and he should have been the one to clean it up. When he thought back on how he had behaved all these years, he was disappointed in himself. It was time to change. This time he'd be the one who set things right.

As he realized what he needed to do, he looked up at the sky. He prayed silently: I know you are up there and always looking out for me, but this time I really need your help. I am really sorry for what I have done. Please let this end safely, especially for my family, and I promise you I will change. TJ closed his eyes tightly for one second. When he opened them the silence was gone and everything was back in motion, including the roar of the blades. His father was furiously shaking his hand to put out the flames, his siblings stared at their father wide-eyed, and his mom and David were trying to remain calm and keep the helicopter stable.

TJ took a deep breath before doing the bravest and scariest thing in his life. Tethered to the helicopter only by the rappel rope, he showed no caution as he went freefalling, head first with his arms flat by his sides, off the edge of the skid and into the blue sky after the eraser. It was terrifying! His body gained speed quickly, but the eraser was still ahead of him. To catch it he would have to go even faster. He moved his arms, positioning his body like an Olympic diver heading into a pool, with his arms leading, and his hands folded together. He was determined to catch the eraser before he ran out of rappel rope. He wasn't sure if it was the laws of physics or his sheer determination that helped him gain speed, but he caught up to the eraser.

He knew he only had one shot at this. If he reached out and missed the eraser, or knocked it in another direction, it would be lost forever in the woods. He continued to plunge downward and, when he was close enough, swung his body toward the eraser, leading with his right arm. He used a swiping motion with his palm open, aiming for the eraser but, instead of catching it, his hand barely tipped the end of it, flipping it up in the air, with his hand coming back, empty. The force of his swing caused his body to continue moving in the direction of the eraser.

TJ cried, "Nooooo!" but suddenly, he closed his mouth to stop the scream.

The upward momentum created by the swing brought TJ back up toward the rappel rope. He was able to twist and thrust his limber body just enough to reach out and catch the rope. Once he had it in his hands, he climbed up toward the chopper. By this time Stephen and Matthew had crawled into the cabin and were lying on their stomachs with hands outstretched to pull TJ inside. The struggle to get back into the chopper got tougher as TJ got closer to the aircraft. He was climbing against the air current from the blades above. Using every reserve of energy, he fought to place one fist over the other. He just had to get a little closer and his brothers could pull him in.

He looked down for a second to see how far away the trees were. Then he felt a hand grab his wrist. As he looked up, he saw his family making a human chain to rescue him. Stephen and Matthew held onto Dad's arm above the burned wrist, and Dad used his good hand to clutch TJ with a tight grip. Even Claudia had taken off her seatbelt to help hold onto her two brothers. On the count of three, everyone used one last burst of energy and pulled TJ in safely.

Dad looked at his son, then at his burned hand, and finally at the picture still strapped to his chest. Above the roar of the blades, he yelled, "Don't worry about the eraser, son, we will think of something. We will find a way to stop the dragon."

At the same time, Stephen and Matthew looked at TJ with sympathy and reached out to hug their brother, letting him know it was okay.

"Listen, man, what you did was totally brave. Dad's right, we will find another way to deal with the dragon," Stephen said.

TJ dropped his chin to his chest in defeat. Realizing everyone felt terrible about the situation, TJ lifted his head and made eye contact with his sister, father and brothers. Then, with a twinkle in his eye, he winked at Claudia and gave a huge grin. There, poking out from between his teeth, was the magic eraser!

When TJ swept his hand to grab the eraser, it flipped up and bounced toward his mouth. Catching the eraser with his teeth was a stroke of genius and a turning point for the Binder Family Mission. Everyone cheered and high-fived TJ; Dad laughed aloud with pride. Without wasting any time, TJ used the rubber finger on the picture. Again, tiny sparks flew from the eraser, but this time the dragon slowly disappeared too. Through binoculars,

Matthew and Stephen watched as the dragon roared it last fiery blast. Finally, the entire image vanished from the paper and the dragon was gone for good. With everyone safely inside the cabin of the helicopter, Mom turned the bird around and headed back to the field.

Mom landed the helicopter with the same precision she had years ago. On the ground, everyone moved quickly to undo telltale signs of the Binder Family Mission before police and other emergency crews showed up. Most importantly, they needed TJ to erase the pictures he had drawn.

TJ started by removing the helicopter. David pleaded for a second to keep the large metal flying machine, but gave up when Mom agreed to let him take flying lessons for his sixteenth birthday.

The equipment was very easy to erase, and TJ worked on deleting all the safety gear, while the remaining Binders got the car loaded. The only image left to deal with was the landscape picture. Sirens in the distance brought everyone to a huddle to decide what to do.

"We could just leave it, you know. It is much nicer than it was before," Mom noted.

"I am just afraid it is evidence that could somehow come back to haunt us," Dad said.

"You're probably right, but I am concerned about how much racket it will make when it gets erased. It felt like an earthquake coming in," Mom reminded her husband.

"All we can do is hope it won't make too much noise, and will be finished changing before the police get here," Dad said. "TJ, start erasing."

TJ started moving the rubber finger across the page. Starting at the very top and using nice even strokes, he slowly erased the beautiful green field. Anticipating the worst, the whole family was surprised to find that the removal was much calmer than the creation of the land. In fact, watching the landscape change was like watching someone roll up a large area rug. The hand-drawn landscape came off the original earth smoothly and evenly. By the time TJ was done erasing the picture, it was impossible to tell that anything had ever taken place in that spot.

Relieved and ready to go home, the Binders piled into the family mini-van and headed out. As they were driving toward the McAllister's farm, a police car arrived and came to a stop, signaling for the Binders to halt. Dad was at the wheel and slowed until his car window was even with the officer's.

"Hi sir, I was wondering if you happened to notice anything going on over here. We received a call from a few folks about a helicopter and some thundering sounds. Ya'll wouldn't happen to know anything about that, huh?" the policeman inquired.

"I'm sorry, officer. I just got out here with my wife and kids, hoping to have a little family picnic. Unfortunately, the mini-van stalled and I clumsily burned my hand on the steam when I removed the radiator cap. Now it looks like we are going to be picnicking at home while I tend to these wounds," he said as he showed the policeman his charred hand.

"Yeow, that looks like a stinger. Ya gotta be careful around a hot engine, you could've really hurt yourself. Well, thanks anyways. You go home and take care of that burn before it gets infected," the officer replied.

"Will do," Dad said as he rolled up his window.

Chapter 17
Home

The Binder family arrived home at 123 Melody Lane exhausted.   They looked as though they had been out on a battlefield for months, instead of in the nearby neighborhood for just the day. Before anyone could sit down and get too comfortable, Dad and Mom ordered all the children upstairs to take a bath and put on pajamas. No one would be going out again for the remainder of the evening.

While the children bathed, Dad got in the car and ran to the pharmacy for ointment and bandages for his hand. He then headed to the hardware store to purchase a heavy duty safe with a combination lock.

TJ was the first kid in and out of the shower, so he was downstairs before his father came home. Knowing his mother was still in her room getting cleaned up, he decided to sit at the kitchen table to relax. That was when he noticed the box of pencils in front of him. He was just thinking that he had no desire to draw anything else for a long time when a sudden thought struck him.

Oh, no, I can't let that happen!

Quickly, he looked around, to be sure no one was watching, then opened the black box and took out a single pencil. He put the lid on the box, hoping he would be able to get the pencil back later without anyone noticing, and headed up the stairs.

When he opened the door to his room, David was putting on his pajamas. Without saying anything, TJ headed over to his desk and took out a piece of paper. He was just starting his picture when David suddenly appeared by his side and snatched the pencil from his hands. "What are you doing?" he asked, looking down at the pencil. "The *Animal* pencil, TJ? What's the matter with you? Didn't you learn anything today? We were all almost killed by that raving lunatic dragon of yours!"

TJ jumped up to get the pencil back, but was not quick enough. "Listen David, you don't understand," he started.

"You're right I don't understand. The pencils are off limits! End of discussion!"

TJ took a deep breath and looked at David pleadingly. "Listen, before all the insanity of dragon, you watched me make that fish tank and those goldfish over there, right?" TJ nodded in the direction of the aquarium on top of their dresser.

"Goldfish are harmless, TJ, but we don't need more of them," said David.

"Will you be quiet for a second and let me finish?" TJ said, worried that he might not get to make one last creation.

"Well, we definitely don't need any more dragons. What else are you planning on doing with this pencil?" David asked.

"Man, you're being bossy and rude. Can I just finish my sentence?" TJ said.

"Fine, ten seconds. What are you doing?" David asked again.

TJ took a second deep breath and explained about the dog he'd made for Claudia. "Man, she will be crushed if she has to go back to sleeping alone again, especially after today. She even named him Magic. I have to draw him again and somehow we have to convince Mom to let her keep him." TJ could tell he had David just about convinced. In addition to feeling bad for Claudia, David loved dogs and would be just as excited as Claudia about having one.

Slowly, David handed the pencil back, saying, "Well, you better hurry, because we have to get the pencil and the dog downstairs before Dad gets back and Mom gets out of the shower."

TJ smiled and sat down at his desk. Just as quickly and nimbly as his fingers had moved with the pencils before, he began sketching the dog. David looked on as TJ worked. Even though he had witnessed the power of the pencils many times before, he still stood by, transfixed as TJ created the dog. Both boys were breathing in slow and steady breaths as TJ drew what would probably be the last creation ever. The image on the paper was complete when suddenly, POOF! There was a medium sized, fluffy brown dog in the middle of the room.

Again, the dog let out a single *rrowf* as soon as his paws hit the floor. He began running in circles in the middle of the room. After a few seconds he started sniffing the ground where the edible fort had rested on the tablecloth. The crumbs had not been vacuumed, and the dog started licking the carpet to pick up tiny morsels of food with his tongue.

"Magic, sit!" TJ commanded.

The obedient dog sat right down, but continued to sniff and lick the carpet.

"He's awesome," David said patting the dog's head. Magic responded by catching David on the face with a big tongue lick.

"He likes you too," TJ said. "Now we just have to figure out how to get him into the back yard without anyone seeing us."

"I'll go downstairs real quick and see if anyone is around," David offered. "Stand by the door so you can hear me call if the coast is clear."

David quickly made his exit and in just a few minutes was back at the foot of the stairs, calling TJ down. David ushered the dog through the kitchen and out the sliding glass door while TJ put the pencil back in the box. Together, they put a bowl of water and some ham out back so the dog would hopefully stay quiet.

Just as they came in after getting Magic settled, Mom came in to the kitchen and Dad came in from the garage. "Honey, are you okay with pizza for dinner tonight? I have no energy for cooking and want to be as far away from heat as possible," Mom remarked.

Before Dad could answer, David and TJ hugged her. "Pizza is great! You're the best mom ever!"

Mom ordered pizza while Dad showered. In the meantime, the other kids came downstairs, cleaned-up and in their pajamas. Together they sat silently on the sofa looking at the TV, but without really watching. The events of the day had been surreal. From the creation of the dragon with magic pencils, to revealing the magic of the pencils to their parents, and ending with TJ's near-death plunge in the skies, the whole thing seemed like a weird dream. Even though they had a lot of questions, no one had the energy to carry on a conversation.

The pizza arrived about the same time Dad came into the kitchen fresh from a shower with his hand neatly bandaged. The family sat at the table together. The aroma of delicious pizza reminded everyone how hungry they really were. The pizza was devoured quicker than usual. With full bellies and exhausted bodies, no one moved. Finally, TJ spoke up. "Mom and Dad, thanks for believing us today and helping with the dragon. You really are great parents, and we all love you."

The others nodded.

Mom looked at them, together and individually. "Listen, I know you rely on each other quite a bit, and that is good, but it is also important to know that when something gets out of hand, you can always come to your father and me. We may not like everything you do, but we love you more than anything else in this world and will always be there to help you. *Capicse*?"

"*Capisce!*" they all replied.

Woof! Magic chimed in from outside on the patio.

"What was that?" Mom asked.

"What was what?" TJ asked back.

Woof, woof!

"That!" Mom said. "It sounds like a dog at our back door."

"A dog! Oh Mom, you know I always wanted a dog!" Claudia exclaimed, jumping from her seat and running to the back door. As she pulled the sliding glass door open, the dog bounced into the house. "Magic!"

"Magic?" Mom repeated, sounding confused. "Do you know this dog, Claudia?"

"No," Claudia replied, thinking quickly. "But he just looks like a Magic, and if I ever got a dog that is what I would name him."

Mom eyed her daughter suspiciously. "Claudia, we cannot keep him. I have told you already, I have no extra time for a dog."

By this time the other children had gotten up from theirs seats and were huddled around the dog, petting him and stroking his fur. "What would you need to do for him, Mom?" David asked. "We would take him out with us every day to play, so he wouldn't need walks."

"And we would bathe him outside," Matthew added.

"And if you increased my allowance I'd buy his food and feed him every day," Stephen offered.

"He could make sure we stay out of trouble, like a watch dog," Claudia chimed in.

"It's not like we're asking to keep a dragon, Mom," TJ said, smiling.

Mom was no match for her family, especially not with the fluffy brown dog sitting there right in front of them. As if to reassure her that keeping him would be the right thing to do, Magic walked over to Mom, lying down by her feet. "Okay, fine," she said. "He seems sweet."

"Really?! We can keep him? Oh Mom, this is the best day of my life!" Claudia exclaimed. "He can sleep in my room! I won't ever complain about sleeping alone again, and I will go to bed early every night!"

Mom smiled. "I guess TJ is right, a sweet dog is much better than an angry dragon."

The children surrounded Magic and leaned over to give him a 'Welcome to the Binder family' hug!

Chapter 18
Promises

A quiet peacefulness had taken over the Binder home. David, Stephen, Matthew were in their beds quietly reading a book. Claudia and Magic were curled up in her bed and sound asleep. TJ came slowly down the stairs. He was thirsty for a glass of milk, but didn't want to disturb anyone. He had turned over a new leaf. From now on he was going to be considerate of others and think about how his behavior would affect them, before he acted foolishly. Tonight he knew his parents probably needed some time alone without being bothered by children. He also reasoned that if his mother was capable of flying a helicopter then he was capable of getting his own glass of milk.

After filling up his glass, he began to head back upstairs. The quiet in the house was only broken by his parent's conversation. He knew it was wrong to eavesdrop, but he thought he heard them talking about the pencils. Hidden from their view by the wall between the stairs and the living room, he listened.

"Well, I think we should just destroy them," said his mother. "Even if they were used for good and not evil, we don't know the long term effects of the images. Suppose everything he draws automatically disappears in ten days, or ten weeks, or ten years? One day we could have our coffee sitting on a coaster on this beautiful new coffee table then suddenly it just vanishes, spilling coffee everywhere. We have no way of predicting the future."

"Honey, with five kids we have no way of predicting the future, even without the pencils," Dad said. "Besides, if you are worried about the coffee table, we can just have TJ erase it, problem solved."

"Not a chance, my friend, I like that coffee table and it is staying. I was just trying to give an example of what could happen," Mom said. "Too many decisions for one day. I guess you are right. We can keep the pencils, but just make sure they stay locked in that safe and TJ *NEVER* gets the combination."

"Agreed. See how easy that is once you admit I am right?" Dad sounded amused. "I will put the safe in the small attic space above our bedroom. The kids don't even know that hiding space exists. Now, for the combination we need five numbers; any ideas?"

"Well we have five kids, so how about using their birthday numbers?" Mom suggested.

"Good idea, that's easy enough. Do you want to use the day or the month?"

Mom thought for a moment. "How about the day for David, TJ, and Claudia, but since Stephen and Matthew have the same birthday we will use both their month and day?"

"Perfect! I will set the numbers starting with David since he is the oldest," Dad said.

Stunned by what he just heard, TJ silently headed upstairs. Now, he not only knew where the pencils were, but the combination code to open the safe. He remembered his promise to think before he acted, but he had to tell someone his secret. David, he thought. He is the perfect person to share this with. He is more sensible and will help keep me from doing anything unwise.

When TJ entered his bedroom, the lights were all out and he could hear David breathing evenly, already in a deep slumber. He thought about how badly he wanted to wake him up and tell him everything he just learned. Then, he thought about the promise he made to be responsible. I can do it, he told himself. I just have to believe in me. Exhausted and achy, he lay down in his bed and drifted off to sleep, hoping his determination to do the right thing would always be stronger than his impulse for mischief.

Acknowledgements

I could not have completed this project without the love, support, and/or inspiration of the following people:

- John and Natalie —You made me who I am. You taught me to believe in myself and to have faith that everything will be okay. I miss you, but know you are still with me.

- Patrick, Davis, and Stephen — Thank you for your understanding and personal sacrifices.

- Stephen, Patrick, and Jamie — Thank you for being the best brothers ever!

- Carol — Your stories of TJ were the inspiration for this book.

- All my students who have provided feedback and encouragement in getting TJ published, especially Campbell, Mallory, Lilah, and Lilly — Thank you!

- Jeff Gunhus, Troon Harrison, and Extended Imagery — Your professional participation is most appreciated.

About the Author

H. Barry Kahl lives outside of Annapolis, Maryland. She enjoys traveling and spending time with family. This is her first novel.

Made in the USA
Middletown, DE
15 June 2018